SWORDS AND SADDLES

ALSO BY JACK CAMPBELL

THE LOST FLEET

Dauntless
Fearless
Courageous
Valiant
Relentless
Victorious

BEYOND THE FRONTIER

Dreadnaught
Invincible
Guardian
Steadfast
Leviathan

THE LOST STARS

Tarnished Knight
Perilous Shield
Imperfect Sword
Shattered Spear

THE ETHAN STARK SERIES

Stark's War
Stark's Command
Stark's Crusade

THE PAUL SINCLAIR SERIES

A Just Determination
Burden of Proof
Rule of Evidence
Against All Enemies

PILLARS OF REALITY

*The Dragons of Dorcastle**
*The Hidden Masters of Marandur**
*The Assassins of Altis**
*The Pirates of Pacta Servanda**
Books 5-6 forthcoming

NOVELLAS

The Last Full Measure

SHORT STORY COLLECTIONS

*Ad Astra**
*Borrowed Time**
*Swords and Saddles**

available as a JABberwocky eBook

SWORDS AND SADDLES

JOHN HEMRY

WRITING AS

JACK CAMPBELL

Published by JABberwocky Literary Agency, Inc.

PUBLICATION HISTORY

"The Rift," first published in *Analog* (October, 2010)

"Swords and Saddles," first published in *Analog* (April 2010)

"Failure to Obey," first published in *Analog* (July/August, 2009)

TABLE OF CONTENTS

AUTHOR'S NOTE
THE RIFT

One of the common assumptions of science fiction and fantasy is that once you know how to communicate with someone (how to speak their language) you will also understand them. Whether they are elves or six-armed aliens from Moduk VI, comprehending what someone means is usually simply a matter of talking to them. That has always bothered me, because among humans even those who share a common language often have trouble understanding each other. What would really happen if humans were dealing with aliens who didn't think like us? How much would the inevitable misunderstandings among the humans hinder grasping the meaning behind the words of the aliens? And what if figuring out the answers was literally a matter of life and death? Those questions are what led to *The Rift*.

THE RIFT

Imtep – Fifth planet from its star. Close to Earth-like (.95 on Ming-Hoffman Scale). Dominated by a single massive continent sprawled across equatorial regions. Eastern areas of the landmass are very rugged, but the central and western regions feature extensive prairies or steppes around a large, shallow inland sea. Native sentient species the Izkop ("People") are humanoid, organized into tribes or clans, the majority living on the plains in agrarian/herder communities. Technology is very limited, primarily craft-metallurgy which allows the construction of durable implements. The Izkop are evaluated as "competitive but non-belligerent," research reports identifying their dominant culture as well-integrated with their environment. A research facility with a staff of eighty has been established on Imtep. Imtep is classified Type Three for human visitation, with pre-clearance required and only small parties allowed to avoid disrupting relations with the native population.

They had to pry Goldera out of the last set of armor when the power pack drained to exhaustion. After forcing open enough of the suit to get Goldera free they left the armor lying there as they resumed walking, the empty carcass sprawled in the short, tough grass like a body denied the benefit of burial. There wasn't any simple way to conceal it, and they lacked the time and the strength to do anything else. The blast rifle, useless without power, lay abandoned alongside the armor.

No one had spoken for at least an hour, everyone concentrating on walking, putting one foot before the other despite the fatigue filling their bodies and minds. Corporal Johansen squinted up at the too-bright sun, trying to remember what had happened over that long day since reveille had sounded at zero three hundred to awaken everyone for the rescue operation. But he couldn't focus on any single, clear memory, his mind filled with disjointed images of the deathtrap which had been a place called Amity.

Johansen brought his gaze down to stare at the back of Sergeant Singh. The sergeant's last spoken command had been "follow me," given as they looked down at a valley where nothing now moved or lived except swarms of Izkop warriors. Since then, Singh had been leading them over the hills around Amity, down through patches of woods and shrubbery, and now across this open area. Fear had lent them speed at first, but now nothing kept them moving except the sergeant's steady pace in front.

With a major effort, Johansen called out just loudly enough for Sergeant Singh to hear. "Sarge."

The sergeant didn't stop, instead turning his upper body and head to look back at the corporal as he kept moving, his face locked into the same expressionless mask as someone under inspection. "Yeah?"

"Gotta rest. They're on their last legs."

"Understood. Not out here." Singh raised one arm to point ahead, toward a tree line. "There. Under cover."

Tall, dark Private Adowa looked toward the trees, her eyes framed by runnels of sweat on her dust-streaked face. "How far is that?"

One corner of Singh's mouth turned upward slowly. "Check the map," his voice grated out sardonically.

The map had been digital, of course, linked to satellite arrays which the Izkop had already shredded. Normally, the soldiers would have called up the map, gotten their precise location, and a precise distance to the trees ahead. But the navigation units had been built into the powered armor, and that was gone along with the sats. All any of the soldiers could do now was look around, inexperienced with judging distances by eye and unaccustomed to marching this far without power assist from their armor.

How far had they come since the dropship set down hard on one side of the valley which had held the human presence on this world? As the platoon had spilled out of the broken dropship they had been presented with a balcony view of the disaster unfolding in the valley itself. Debris from what been the buildings of the human civilian community still falling back to the surface, craters marking the graves of damaged dropships which had plowed in too hard for any survivors, elsewhere scattered groups of soldiers firing frantically at the masses of Izkop swarming over the entire valley floor. More Izkop popped up, among and all around the platoon, their heavy spears flashing in the light of the morning sun, surging into the dropship to wipe out the crew, dragging down soldiers and tearing apart the robotic mules carrying the backup power packs. Sergeant Singh had rallied them, tried to get as many soldiers as he could up the side of the valley, while everyone shot as fast as they could and members of the platoon got swamped one by one.

Where had all of the aliens come from? Somebody had been screaming "out of the ground" on the comm circuit before their signal cut off.

Johansen focused on that puzzle to distract himself from the fatigue that threatened to overwhelm him. *Out of the ground.* He hadn't had much time to look around during the fight. None of them had. But he recalled visions of slabs of turf lying neatly cut and overturned. "The ground," he muttered. "The bastards were all lying under the sod."

Private Stein turned partway to frown at Johansen, then his

expression cleared with understanding. "That's where they came from? Because nobody said anything going in. Landing fields are clear, they said."

Adowa shook her head. "They also said we should be careful not to cause any violent reaction by the Izkop. Just a rescue and security op in a 'possibly non-permissive environment.' Possibly non-permissive, hell. Orbital sensors can't see aliens lying under a layer of dirt and grass, ready to kill us as we hit dirt."

"What did the damned civilians do to make the Izkop want to wipe out everyone and us in the bargain?" Private Nassar wondered. "The Izkop didn't care how many of them we killed."

Only Private Burgos answered, her eyes haunted. "We didn't kill enough," she whispered.

They fell silent again after that, just trying to keep moving in the wake of the sergeant, who plowed onward as if he himself were a suit of armor with an inexhaustible power supply. Johansen looked backwards at times, fearing to see the shapes of Izkop coming after them, and irrationally hoping that other soldiers would appear to join them. But he saw nothing, though as the march went on under the blazing sun Johansen sometimes imagined others marched with them, seeing the shapes of soldiers he had once known wavering insubstantially until he blinked and shook his head to clear it. The tree line gradually grew closer, resolving into a thin forest which would offer at least a little cover from the Izkop and a little shade from the sun.

Singh kept them going after they reached the first trees, onward about a hundred meters, before he stumbled to a halt. "Rest. Half an hour."

The others didn't so much sit down as drop, collapsing in place with expressions of mingled pain and relief. Johansen let himself fall as well, luxuriating in not having to keep moving, but after a few minutes forced himself to struggle up until he sat with his back against a tree. *Second in command. You're second in command now.* The lieutenant was dead, the other sergeants were dead, and so were the other corporals. For that matter, so was the colonel and everybody else ranking higher than the sergeant. *Hell, I'm second in command of the entire relief force now. All eight of us that are left.*

Eight out of a little more than two hundred in the battalion.

Johansen looked at the six privates who had made it out of the valley with him and Singh. Goldera, short, lean and wiry, lay on his back, staring blankly upward. Adowa, her dark face and hair blending a bit into the shadows beneath the trees, had a jaw slack with fatigue, but her eyes kept roaming the woods, on watch for danger. Archer, one of the worst shots in the unit despite her name, was a bit smaller than Goldera but had clung stubbornly to the platoon's portable long-range comm unit despite its weight and now lay hugging it to her chest with both arms. Nassar sat limply against a tree, but like Adowa his eyes were still alert and searching the woods around them, the buzz-saw light machine gun resting on his lap. Stein, big and solid, lay as if dead, only the movement of his chest revealing that he still lived. Burgos, her eyes open but glazed, seemed to still be looking at the deadly chaos around Amity and unaware of their current surroundings.

Sergeant Singh had lowered himself to sit, breathing deeply, his eyes hooded in thought as if they were just on some especially difficult training mission and the sergeant had to figure out how to beat a tough scenario.

As if sensing Johansen's gaze, Singh nodded to him. "Now that we've reached cover we'll rest ten minutes each hour after we get going again."

News which normally would have been greeted with muttered complaints from the tired privates brought nothing this time, a measure of their utter exhaustion, but Adowa stopped scanning the woods long enough to look at Singh. "Where are we going?"

Singh jerked his head in the direction they had been traveling since leaving the valley. "Before my armor gave out I spotted a place on the map. A small outpost of some kind along a river. At least one permanent building. We're sure to hit the river if we keep going this way. Then we find that outpost."

"Water," Stein mumbled. "River's got water."

"Yeah. And maybe there's food at that outpost," Johansen said. They hadn't carried much, just the usual emergency packs. The other rations had been destroyed with the dropships.

"We hope," Singh replied. "And maybe some shelter. Depends what the Izkop did to it." He didn't have to elaborate. Much of Amity had been intact when the dropships launched, but just before the Izkop erupted out of the soil they had blown apart all of the buildings, taking soldiers and dropships with them.

Nassar breathed out slowly. "Someplace safe, maybe."

Adowa shook her head. "Safe? How many Izkop got to be looking for us, Sarge? There were thousands back there, and they know we got clear."

"We haven't seen them following us yet," Johansen said.

"We didn't see them in the valley, either, until we did. How much trouble would they have tracking us with eight suits of armor laying dead, pointing this way? Any fool could follow us."

"Maybe" Archer murmured, "they couldn't keep up. Sarge moved us a long ways pretty quick."

This time Nassar shook his head. "You heard the briefings. 'On open ground, the Izkop are very fast and can maintain their speed over long distances,'" he quoted. "They may not be big like Stein, but they're strong enough. Why did we get this far?"

Everyone looked at Sergeant Singh, who shrugged. "No idea. Shooting our way out of the valley wasn't a low profile op, and they nailed everyone else who was trying to get out in other directions."

"So," Adowa insisted, "why didn't they run us down?"

"They didn't want to lose any more of their own?" Goldera asked.

Nassar snorted. "You saw them swarm everyone down in the

valley. No concern with casualties at all. If we hadn't burned out the suits so fast, firing the energy weapons without a break and jumping up one side of those hills and down the other as fast as we could, we'd be back there with everyone else, getting our guts hauled out and danced on. It's a miracle we made it this far."

Burgos roused enough to glare at Nassar. "I'm not dying before I kill a lot more of them."

The sergeant eyed her soberly. "Ramada's dead. We need to stay alive."

"Yeah." Burgos barely whispered as she closed her eyes again, shuddering slightly, her left hand clasped tightly so the ring on it stood out clearly.

After a moment of silence, Nassar spoke. "They were waiting for us. How long did they just lay there, under the turf, waiting for us to come down?"

"Days," Adowa said. "Crazy bastards. How do you plan for fighting against something that'd lay that kind of ambush? I got to tell you, I'm worried we left someone. Somebody still alive."

"Us being dead wouldn't keep them alive," Johansen said.

Archer sat up wearily, brushing hair from her face with one hand and nodding toward the portable comm unit. "I've heard no signals from anyone else living since we got clear. For a while I kept picking up automatic distress signals from armor back at Amity, reporting occupants Killed In Action. No wounded needing pickup, just KIAs. But the KIA signals went off, I guess when the Izkop got around to smashing them. I can understand the Izkop pulling the bodies out of the armor, but why go to so much trouble to smash all the equipment on the armor, too, even while the fight was still going on?"

"I guess we can't ask the civs we were supposed to be rescuing," Adowa said. "Wonder how long they've all been dead and if they put up any fight?"

The sergeant shrugged again. "Probably a while and probably

not. The civs here were just researchers. Their reports on file didn't pay much attention to Izkop fighting methods."

Johansen snorted. "The civ reports barely mentioned that the Izkop had spears. What did the civs call the Izkop? Competitive?"

"And non-belligerent. I keep getting the feeling they're out there," Goldera added. "Watching us. Sure wish I still had the scout sensors in my armor."

"There's a lot of stuff in the armor we'll miss, but good soldiers can fight without it," Singh said. He focused on Archer again. "Are you sure the comm unit didn't take any damage?"

Archer smiled slightly and stroked the outside of the comm unit. "Aimee's fine. Ready to talk when we find someone to talk to. The solar collectors on her shell can keep her charged indefinitely and recharge batteries for any other gear we've got left."

"Too bad it couldn't recharge the armor," Goldera grumbled. "They took out the big ship. How the hell did they know how to take out the ship? Primitives, hell."

"They used the research facility's own protective system," Johansen said. "The *Sara* wasn't ready."

"Nobody was," Nasser observed. "The Izkop burned out everything taking down the ship and our dropships and frying a lot of the satellite arrays and blowing up everything in that valley. Why'd the Izkop kill all the civs, anyway?" he asked again.

"Who cares why?" Burgos had both hands on her rifle. The lightweight slug throwers, emergency weapons usually stowed literally up on the back of the armor, had become their primary means of defense now. "Murdering scum. Their reasons don't matter."

"Yes, they do," Singh corrected. "Understanding the enemy is critical. If we don't understand them, we don't know what they might do next." The sergeant had always worn an old-fashioned watch, not depending on suit systems to keep him aware of the time as most others did. Now he consulted it. "On your feet everybody. We've got a ways to go."

They staggered onward, the sergeant always in the lead, Johansen always at the rear to make sure everyone stayed with them. There were plenty of times when he wondered if he would collapse as the too-long day on this planet kept the sun crawling slowly through the sky, beating brutally down on them even through the scattered screen of shade provided by the trees. But if he fell out somebody else might drop and be lost, too. So he kept going.

The river proved just as impossible to miss as the sergeant had predicted, meandering across their path, perhaps fifty meters wide but apparently shallow all the way across. As everyone drank their fill through filter straws, Singh studied the terrain. "The map showed some ridges on either side of the place we're looking for."

Johansen looked up and down the stream. "The bluffs beside the river course are just mounds along here. It looks like they're higher upstream."

"Yeah." Sergeant Singh gazed up at the sun. "I figure we've maybe two hours of sunlight left."

"The night vision gear was all built into the armor."

"Yeah," Singh repeated. "We don't want to be stumbling around in the dark. Let's get moving, people. We need a place to fort up by nightfall."

As they moved back into the tree line, Goldera paused to look around.

"You see anything?" Johansen asked him.

"Nah. Haven't seen anything but what passes for birds and squirrels here." Goldera hesitated, scanning the horizon. "Still feels like they're out there, though."

"Keep an eye out," Johansen said, then moved alongside Singh long enough to pass on what Goldera had said. Singh only grunted in reply, and Johansen fell back again as the tiny column reached the trees and then turned to move upstream.

They found it when the sun was only a short ways above the horizon. The bluffs on either side of the river's lowland had risen enough to form a rift between them. The woods dwindled near the edge of the rift, leaving an area almost open along the sides before the land fell away abruptly into bottomland with the river snaking along roughly through the center. Singh and the others wormed forward on their bellies toward one edge of the rift until Singh could raise his field glasses to examine the small cluster of buildings constructed to human standards, while they all lay as concealed as possible by the sparse vegetation.

After a moment, the sergeant cursed softly and lowered the glasses. "Power focus. Great stuff until the power dies. Anybody got charged batteries?"

Without rising, Archer held out one hand toward Burgos, who took what she held and passed it to Stein, who handed the batteries to Johansen who gave them to Singh. After the sergeant replaced the batteries in his field glasses, he passed the worn out batteries from them back along the chain until Archer got them and slid them into charging slots on her comm unit.

Focusing again, Singh stayed motionless for a long time, then finally passed the glasses to Johansen. "What do you think?"

Johansen focused, trying not to expose himself too much to any watchers. "It looks intact." The compound was dominated by a low-slung one-story structure that apparently combined living quarters and offices. From here that main building looked substantial, with thick walls of compressed dirt and a heavy roof of reinforced metal with built-in solar cells. The rest of the buildings, including a small livestock shed, were of much simpler construction, just stamped metal set on concrete pads.

"See any sign of Izkop?"

"No. No sign now, and no sign they've been there. Maybe once the civs left the Izkop didn't bother with it." One of the doors to the main building swung idly in the wind. "It looks abandoned…or someone wants it to look abandoned."

Something moved among the buildings and Johansen stiffened as he watched, the others falling into tense silence. As the thing moved fully into sight, Johansen almost laughed with relief. "A cow. There's still a cow alive down there."

"A cow." Singh made it a statement, gesturing for the return of the field glasses, then studied the animal. "A cow," he confirmed, lowering the glasses. "Not one of the local herd beasts. A milk cow, Earth-livestock."

"Milk?" Adowa did laugh very softly, her face lowered into the dirt to muffle the sound. "Too bad I'm lactose intolerant."

Singh didn't smile in return. "A milk cow. Abandoned here. It wouldn't have been milked for some time. But it seems content."

"You know cows, Sarge?" Goldera asked.

"My family's neighbors had some." Singh looked at Johansen. "After only a few days, an unmilked cow would be very uncomfortable."

"Somebody's been milking it?"

"Yes. Would an Izkop do that? Could an Izkop do that without the cow panicking? Stein, didn't your family have a ranch?"

"Yeah, Sarge." Stein's large face creased slowly in thought. "No. If what the briefers told us is right, cows wouldn't like the Izkop, and cows can be damned skittish even with people."

"Could there still be people down there?" Archer asked.

"Either there are, or it's another Izkop trap," Johansen said. "You've still got nothing on the comm unit?"

"No. If any civs survived, they're staying silent."

Singh looked back at them all. "We go down there, or we go on."

"Go on? Where?" Nassar wondered.

"Nothing any better than this, and nothing we can reach with less than another full days walk, *if* we could find it."

Johansen sighed and checked his weapon. "I'm getting tired of walking, and it'll be dark soon. We might as well see what's here."

Burgos licked her lips, her eyes fever bright. "If there's Izkop, maybe it's just a small force. We can wipe them out."

Singh pointed one finger at her. "Or there's ten thousand of them within sound of a shot. Nobody fires without my orders."

"Yeah, Sarge," Burgos muttered, her expression sullen.

"You go spindizzy on me and I'll shoot you myself, got it?" Singh kept his eyes on her, hard and demanding.

Burgos flushed. "I said yes, sergeant."

Fortunately, the compound was on this side of the river so they didn't have to splash through the water and mud. Tired as they were, the soldiers still moved carefully toward the buildings, only two moving at a time while the others covered them. Once inside the bluffs the flatland around the river was covered with short, round bushes with sparse leaves that caused Stein to mutter "tumbleweeds," but the area inside the human-built compound had only short grass growing.

Johansen came up against the main building, his rifle at ready, his back to the wall right next to the open doorway where the door still swung lazily in occasional gusts of wind. Adowa crouched on the other side of the door, raising her weapon questioningly. Johansen shook his head, then looked back to where Singh and the others were lying in the grass, their weapons aimed at the windows and doors of the building. He pulled out his combat knife, took a deep breath to fight down a wave of fear, then spun around the corner and inside, once again planting his back against the wall with the knife at the ready before him.

A figure moved, jerking to one side with a gasp of fright. Johansen swung the knife's point that way even as his mind shouted *human*. "Who are you?" Johansen demanded.

Instead of replying to his question, the figure rose, resolving into a woman who stared at him in disbelief. "Are you a soldier?"

"Yes, ma'am. Any Izkop here?"

"No." She looked anguished for a moment, then swallowed and steadied. "We haven't seen any here since the recall. We've been unable to contact Amity since then." Her expression changed. "We heard what sounded like explosions in the distance this morning. In the direction of Amity."

Johansen just nodded. "We? You're not alone here?"

"No. There's two other adults and ten children. The others are in the back rooms."

Finally relaxing, Johansen leaned out the door to wave an all clear and beckon to the others.

The other soldiers came on carefully, still dodging forward until each darted inside the doorway. As he waited for them and watched for trouble, Johansen saw that the building's interior consisted of a big main room which stretched all the way across its width and perhaps a third of the way back, where an inside wall showed hallways and doors leading to what must be living quarters and offices. A series of big windows ran along the front and partway down the sides, but only two doors were visible, the main entry and a side door. The tables and chairs inside had been pushed around, and the big flat display on the back wall sat dark and silent. Singh entered last, studying the room somberly.

The woman had gone to the back and came out again with two other civilians, both men, one young and the other well past middle-age. "I'm Ariana Tisrok," she said. "This is Juni Garios and Scorse Kalinga."

"Sergeant Singh," he introduced himself. "Suppose you tell us what happened here?"

Ariana slumped into a chair. "We don't know much."

The younger man named Juni nodded. "We received the recall. Everybody was to report back to Amity on an emergency basis. But the truck we have here was out on a research run." He hesitated, his eyes going to Ariana, then Scorse. "It had, um, four people with it."

"Including my husband," Ariana said in a low voice. Taking a deep breath, she continued. "We tried calling our truck. Nothing. We tried getting a fix on its position, but the transponder was out. It should have been back before sundown that day but it never showed. We called Amity, to tell them we needed a ride and asking for more details. We never heard any reply. My – the people with the truck would have been able to walk back here within a day if it had broken down."

"Our truck might've made it to Amity," Scorse said stubbornly. "My wife –" He stopped talking for a moment. "They might have made it to Amity," he repeated, the simple statement sounding like a prayer.

"What reason did Amity give for the recall?" Singh asked.

The researchers exchanged glances. "Something about crowds of Izkop. Large numbers of them," Juni finally offered. "'Tribal situation uncertain.' That was the last thing I heard."

"What were you supposed to do if the Izkop turned hostile?"

"Hostile?"

"Yes," Singh said patiently. "If the Izkop attacked, what were you supposed to do?"

"The Izkop attacked?" Ariana asked.

Johansen didn't quite suppress an inarticulate grunt of disbelief at the question. Rather than answer Ariana directly, Singh pointed upward. "The regional base at Mandalay, about ten light years from here, got an emergency pulse from the human base on this planet through the quantum entanglement comms. Those can't provide details, but it was the most urgent emergency pulse that could be sent, the one that calls for military assistance as quickly as possible. We're from the on-call battalion at Mandalay. They loaded us on the *Saratoga* and we jumped here. Once inside the star system we started picking up messages your people had begun sending over a week before, talking about danger from the Izkop and requesting emergency protection."

The three civilians looked at each other in amazement, then Juni faced Singh again. "We never heard those messages. Not long after the recalls, the satellite relays went down, and without those we haven't been able to pick up anything."

"You don't have an emergency transmitter/receiver?" Archer asked.

"Yes, but –" Juni gave the other civilians an embarrassed look.

"It was stored in one of the sheds. Everything in that shed got ransacked and smashed the night after we heard the recall, before we knew the relays were down."

"So the Izkop know you're here?" Johansen asked.

"We don't know that the Izkop were responsible for that."

"Who else could have done it?" Ariana asked. "The Izkop knew we were here then. In the days since we've tried to make it look like we left, because…there wasn't much else we could do."

"And because you insisted on it," Juni grumbled.

"If we'd been alone," Scorse said, "we'd have set out for Amity on foot, but not with ten *children* to worry about."

"Ten children?" Singh asked. "Are they all yours?"

"None of them are ours. It was a field trip," Ariana explained. "Normally we wouldn't have children here. They were staying for a few nights."

"No other adults or transport with them?"

"The two adults escorting the children were also out with our truck. An all-terrain bus brought the children in and was supposed to pick them up three days later. It's not that long a drive from Amity."

Adowa, who had been leaning against one wall peering suspiciously out a window, now looked at Ariana. "It's a long walk. How many kids were still in Amity?"

"None. A few teens. All of the preteens are here."

"The Izkop hit the valley while all the kids were here?"

"I suppose - Hit?" Ariana stared at Adowa, then at Singh. "The Izkop attacked Amity?"

All of the other soldiers looked at Sergeant Singh, who exhaled heavily before replying. "Yes."

"Did they kill anyone?"

Burgos made a choking sound.

Singh nodded twice. "There's nothing left living at Amity except Izkop. Lots of Izkop. They blew up the buildings there, they self-destructed the equipment, and they seem to have burnt out everything in orbit."

None of the civilians spoke for a long moment. Ariana recovered first. "They're…all…dead?"

"Yes, ma'am. As far as we know, the only humans left alive on this planet are in this building."

"I…I don't…" Juni made a baffled gesture. "If the Izkop are that dangerous, why did your commander only send eight of you here? And on foot?"

The sergeant spoke carefully. "I said every human still alive is here. We're all that's left of our unit. The Izkop were waiting for us. They turned your systems on us and took down the big ship that brought us, as well as about half the dropships carrying us to the surface. Half the battalion died that way. The Izkop swarmed the other dropships and anyone who got out onto the surface. Nobody had time to form up before they got overrun, so our individual fire-power advantage wasn't enough."

The civs fell silent again. Juni just sat as if unable to absorb the news. Ariana kept blinking back tears. Scorse put his face in his hands, shuddering with what seemed like anger rather than grief, then shot to his feet, his eyes blazing. "You got away!" Scorse accused. "How the hell did *you* get away? You just ran, didn't you? You left everyone else to die and –"

He stopped talking as the barrel of Burgos' rifle came to rest a millimeter from his nose. "Shut up," she breathed.

"Private Burgos." Singh's voice was calm and authoritative. "Stand down."

She held the weapon in the man's face a moment longer, then stepped back, lowering it. "If you say that again, I'll kill you," she told Scorse in a cold voice. "We fought."

"*Stand down,*" Singh repeated. "Sir, I would strongly advise you not to question the courage of my soldiers. We left most of our platoon dead and barely shot our own way out of there. There was nothing else we could have done but die on the spot. Now, if we're lucky, we'll be able to hold out here until another ship gets in. When the *Saratoga* doesn't send a routine status pulse back to Mandalay they should send another ship to check on things. If we're lucky, someone could be here in a week."

"And if we're not lucky?" Juni asked.

"Then we're all dead," Adowa said. Singh glared at her but she just bared her teeth in a fierce, humorless smile. "They ought to know, Sarge."

Ariana shook her head, her expression torn between grief and denial. "How could it have happened? If the Izkop pressed us, we were to withdraw. Pull back from contact until the misunderstanding or whatever was resolved. They knew we weren't here to stay, to colonize or conquer."

"Maybe some of the Izkop didn't get the word on that," Nassar commented from his watch post near another window.

Singh gave him a flat look which shut up Nassar, then turned back to the civilians. "How many Izkop have you seen around here?"

"The first day after the recall, we observed a few," Juni offered in the voice of a man coming out a daze. "Out in the hills, while we were looking to see if the truck was coming in. Before that, there'd been a lot of Izkop movement. The satellites tracked many Izkop moving toward Amity."

"Didn't that worry anybody?"

"There were varying interpretations about the meaning of the Izkop movements. I...don't know what they did at Amity," Juni mumbled.

Singh leveled a finger at Goldera. "It's almost sunset. Get out there and do a scout while we've still got some light. Nassar, watch his back. I want to know what you see around this place, especially whether there's signs that the Izkop are watching it."

"Okay, Sarge." Goldera slipped out the door, followed a moment later by Nassar.

Singh sat down, gesturing this time to Johansen and Adowa.

"Keep an eye on the outside. Burgos, you and Stein check out this compound. Carefully and quietly. I want to know how it looks from a defensive standpoint. *No firing at anything.* Archer, run a full diagnostic on that comm unit. That's our only lifeline for calling the relief ship when it gets here. Nothing better happen to it. Now, I understand you civilians have been in for an awful shock, but I'd like a better idea of what happened. Are you sure you don't have any idea why the Izkop went spindizzy?"

"No," Juni said, hunched over as he sat staring at his hands. "What you describe is uncharacteristic. The Izkop have ceremonies which to outside observers can replicate aggression, but they haven't shown any radical deviations from standard behavioral modes."

"Ceremonies. They haven't been acting aggressive?"

"No. Not that I've heard or observed. The Izkop are well integrated into their environment and have no need to manifest authentic belligerent group behaviors."

Ariana shook her head. "I believe the Izkop are an actively aggressive culture, but they haven't acted aggressively toward us. There's been some pushing of our limits, but nothing serious."

Singh raised one eyebrow. "Pushing your limits?"

"In terms of our equipment, asking more about it. At first they wouldn't ask at all, then gradually they got more interested and wanted to know more. Over time we'd show them a little more, to build bonds of trust and ensure they knew these were simply technological devices."

"They haven't pushed," Juni objected. "They just ask. They're manifesting natural curiosity about new factors in their environment."

"What about when you said no?" Singh asked. "How did the Izkop react to that?"

Ariana spread her hands helplessly. "I doubt anyone ever simply said no. We're researchers. We've been trained in nonviolent conflict resolution. When the Izkop press us on something we divert them or find a way to address their concerns or whatever is necessary to keep the situation from escalating."

"And you had no indications that wasn't working?" Singh questioned. "Let me tell you what we heard on the way in. The civilians in Amity were sending out messages, both general emergency signals and specific calls for help. They showed video of large numbers of Izkop carrying spears surrounding that valley where your main settlement was located."

"Amity isn't a settlement," Juni corrected. "It's a research installation."

"Fine. According to these messages, lots of Izkop were threatening the humans there. The same few messages kept auto-repeating. Now we know that must have been because the humans who sent them were already dead. Then the messages cut off after the first transmissions from our ship reached the planet. We figured the Izkop must have trashed the transmitters somehow to keep the humans here from replying to us, but actually the Izkop apparently just killed the signals once they knew we were being lured in."

"You're assuming a rather high level of sophistication in their planning of an act of violence," Juni said. "How could the Izkop have learned how to take those actions and plan such an entrapment?"

Ariana turned an angry look on him. "Their legends are full of accounts of battles and ambushes."

"Literary and historical-cultural inheritances can't realistically be employed to put into practice major changes in group inter-relational dynamics."

"The Izkop knew what they were doing," Johansen said. "Not only did they lay a near-perfect ambush for us, but someone showed them how to handle a lot of the equipment there, and they figured out how to modify functions to use non-weapons as weapons."

"Everything we have is user friendly," Ariana said in a low voice. "It's not that hard for anyone to grasp. All you need to do is navigate through simple touch menus to change settings. But at this outpost we never showed the Izkop much. Just the simplest things."

"And in Amity?" Singh asked.

"They…might have been forced to show more. A great deal more. If the Izkop threatened them. What you're describing seeing sounds like a dominance display."

Singh sat back, glancing at Johansen. "What's your opinion?"

"We're still missing a reason."

"Yeah."

His eyes glowing with rage, Scorse shouted at them. "They wanted our equipment and they were willing to kill for it! I know soldiers like you don't come from the best and brightest, but how hard is that to figure out?"

Singh kept his own voice dispassionate. "If the Izkop wanted your equipment, sir, why did they blow it all to hell?"

Scorse got up without replying and stormed into another part of the building.

Ariana spoke in a choked voice. "You're certain everyone else is dead?" Singh nodded, somber again. "Juni, could you look after the children alone for a few minutes?" She excused herself and also went off by herself, while Juni scowled and headed to a back room where the children must be.

"Lost her husband," Adowa said in the silence after the civilians left. "Too bad we had to tell her."

"We didn't have a chance to save him," Johansen said, knowing he sounded defensive.

"No. I'm just saying. Hard to hear, you know?"

"Yeah." Scorse had lost his spouse as well, but cruel as it might be Johansen couldn't muster up the same sympathy. Johansen looked around again as Juni led out from the back room a small column of children.

"See," the young man told the children, "these soldiers are here now."

The soldiers nodded to the kids, who nodded solemnly back, their eyes big. "Are you taking us back to Amity?" one who looked about ten years old asked.

"No," Singh said. "We'll be leaving on a ship with…everyone on the planet."

"Why are you here?"

"Why are we leaving?"

"Why can't we call home?"

"Where's my mom and dad?"

Singh hesitated, uncharacteristically uncertain, so Johansen forced a smile, standing up to convey genial authority. "Hey, guys, we're just soldiers here to do our jobs. You got your people here like Juni. They'll tell you anything they can, but right now a lot of it is secret. You understand?" The children nodded reluctantly, while Juni kept his eyes averted from them. "So you guys stay in the back. That's part of the secret. You have to keep hidden back there until the ship gets here. Okay?"

The children still looked doubtful. "But we've been in there for a loooong time," one complained. "*Days*. And we hardly ever get to come out."

Archer smiled, too, as she winked conspiratorially at them. "We need your help guys. This is a special game, like my buddy there says. Stay secret, stay hidden, stay cool." The extra maternal boost must have been enough, because the kids smiled back and nodded.

Juni hesitated, then herded the kids into the back again, leaving the soldiers looking at each other.

"Thanks, Johansen. Thanks, Archer," Singh said.

"Nyet problema, Sarge." Archer gave the inner door a puzzled look. "Why'd he bring them out here? Like he was trying to dump them on us."

"He hasn't got kids of his own," Adowa said. "You can tell. And he's really shook up by this. He didn't say it like the old son of a bitch did, but he's another one of those guys who think because they spent ten years in college they understand everything."

Johansen nodded. "Only he's realizing that he can't understand this. The real world is always a shock, but this is a lot worse than those guys usually deal with, and all he can do is take care of the kids.."

"Well, I'd love to help," Archer said, "but I got other things to do right now, and he doesn't."

"You can bet he realizes that, too, and isn't too thrilled to know it."

A few minutes later Burgos and Stein came back, Burgos shaking her head. "Just empty sheds out there. There's hay in a small barn for the cow. Nothing we can use. That shed where they had their emergency gear was completely trashed. Nothing usable in it. Why the hell didn't they have that stuff in here with them?"

Singh waved around. "Living quarters. You should know some of that survival gear isn't allowed to be stowed in living areas. Flares and stuff, because of the hazard. How's the back of this place look?"

"Solid wall. Maybe bad storms always come from that way. The sides of the building back from here have a couple of doors we need to seal off, but the only windows in those areas are slits high up. If we guard the front and sides of this room we'll be okay, though the Izkop could dig through at other places in time." She sat down, holding her rifle across her chest, her expression gloomy.

"The civs have been milking that cow," Stein offered. "Feeding it hay, too."

"The Izkop would have spotted that if there's any around," Singh said, then looked over as Goldera and Nassar returned. "What'd you see?"

Goldera swung his arm in a wide arc through the east, north and west. "They're out there, Sarge. I knew it. Lots of them. I could see groups of Izkop scattered all around in those directions. None of them seemed to be focused on here, but they were out there all over the place. Not real easy to see, either. I could only spot them when they moved. But it looked clear to the south."

"Clear?" Singh questioned.

"Yeah, Sarge. Not an Izkop in sight that way. There's decent cover and the terrain's easy. We could move fast."

Singh leaned back, frowning, then glanced at Johansen.

Johansen didn't hesitate. "Too easy." Like the landing zone had looked.

"That's what I was thinking," Singh said. "That good cover to the south could be hiding Izkop who *aren't* moving. Still, they might be expecting us to be keeping to the rougher territory, and there was another research outpost northwest of here they might think we were aiming for."

This time Johansen gestured toward the back of the house. "Those kids couldn't move fast. If it was just us, maybe. But not with them."

"Yeah, that pretty much settles it, doesn't it?" Singh looked out of the closest window. "Even if it's clear to the south, we can't go without leaving the civs here to the Izkop."

"It's a chance," Goldera insisted. "Maybe our only chance to live."

Adowa gave him a hard look. "We've seen those kids. You should take a look, too. How you going to live knowing you left them to the Izkop?"

"That's the thing," Singh agreed. "We came here to protect the civs. It looks like these are the only civs left, so I figure we have to stay here and protect them."

"But staying here won't make any difference," Goldera protested. "I wasn't talking about leaving anybody, just us *all* making a run for it. I won't leave any kids."

"They couldn't keep up." Singh looked around. "So we hold here as long as we can, soldiers. Let's get things set up for a siege. None of us were high enough in the food chain to know how close other ships are, or what time the *Sara* was supposed to send in her status pulse each day. Another ship might already be on the way, might get here in time to lift us all out, if we hold out long enough. Make sure those back doors are sealed and that there's no other ways in."

When Ariana returned, her eyes reddened but her expression determined, they tallied up the food resources at the outpost. "With you here as well as the children," she said, "we probably have about six days worth of food left. We've already been cut off for a while and we're not set up for this population."

"What about the cow?" Stein asked. "She's pretty well-fed. Lot of meat on her. I can do the butchering."

Ariana gave him a wan look. "The cow is…was…an experiment, to see how the Izkop would react to her. We were hoping…her milk has helped stretch our supplies."

"I understand, ma'am," Stein assured her. "A milk-cow isn't like a beef animal. People get attached to them. But it looks like we'll need that meat."

"We wait six days," Singh decided. "On the seventh day, if no relief ship has shown up, we kill the cow." The sergeant stood up, stretching, much harder to see as darkness fell rapidly with the disappearance of the sun. "We're all exhausted, too tired to keep talking tonight, but the Izkop are out there. We stand watches, two hours each, until sunrise. You handle the schedule, Johansen. Make sure the sentries know not to show themselves and not to show any lights, and to wake the rest of us if they hear anything even if it doesn't sound dangerous."

"Yes, sergeant."

Johansen saw and heard nothing unusual during his portion of the watch that night. None of the others reported detecting activity, either. But at dawn Johansen was awakened by a string of curses recited in a monotonous tone by Singh. "What happened?"

"Take a look," Singh offered, beckoning out the window he was kneeling beside with Burgos, who had the last watch. "Everybody else, get up now!"

Raising himself cautiously, Johansen felt a pit open inside him as he looked at what the dawn's light had revealed. The area around the compound and for about five hundred meters beyond was empty, but outside that what seemed to be a solid mass of Izkop stood in apparently endless ranks, spears in their hands, gazing silently at the human building. Like the Izkop they had fought in the valley, these wore no armor, just odd pants which came only partway down the upper legs and partway up the abdomen.

"I didn't hear *anything*," Burgos said, her hands twisting on her rifle as she stared at the Izkop.

"Nobody heard anything," Singh replied. "Or saw anything. These guys are very good at concealment, but we're also too used to depending on the sensors in the armor to hear and see trouble."

Ariana gazed out with a hopeless expression, Juni seemed puzzled as well as frightened, while Scorse glared hatred.

The other soldiers took positions at the windows, weapons ready. Most of them simply muttered despairing curses, but after Stein had gazed out for a while he looked troubled. "Sarge?" he questioned. "There's a lot of them. I don't think we got enough ammo."

Adowa started laughing, then Johansen joined in, then Archer, Goldera and Nasser. Even Singh laughed, and finally Stein added his hoots to the mix. Only Burgos sat silent, as well as all of the civilians, who were now watching the soldiers in amazement.

"Why are you laughing?" Juni finally asked.

That just made them laugh again, loud and long, even Burgos gasping a few bitter snorts, Johansen himself feeling the darkness inside, the certainty of doom which only dark, irrational humor could keep at bay. He noticed that Singh had stopped laughing, though, and was gazing thoughtfully out the window. "What's up?"

"They're listening," Singh commented as the last chuckles died away. "You could tell they were listening to us laugh, and watching us. Do the Izkop understand human laughter?" he asked Ariana.

"Yes," she said, hurrying to look out the window beside the sergeant. "They have a capacity for mirth that seems similar to our own though I don't understand any of their jokes. I can't tell from here how they're reacting to your laughter. Their facial muscles don't show emotions in the same ways ours do, so it wouldn't be easy even if we were closer." Ariana sat back, her eyes now on the soldiers. "That display. It's meant to impress. To frighten enemies. But you all *laughed*."

"Is that going to make them mad?" Adowa asked sarcastically.

"There's an Izkop phrase that I think translates as 'greeting death with smiles.' They use it in their legends, to describe heroes." Ariana took another cautious look outside. "See those Izkop gathered together, the ones with the tattoos and decorations? Those are leaders. They're talking, and I'm sure it's about you laughing when they expected you to be overawed."

"Let's give them something else to talk about," Nassar suggested, hefting the buzz-saw. "Hey!" he called. "Whenever you're ready! Come and get it!"

"Quiet," Singh ordered. "Ma'am, do you know them well enough to see if they'll talk to you? Maybe arrange a truce or something?"

Ariana hesitated. "I don't know if they'll – What did they do at Amity? To…everyone else? Did they just kill them or…?"

Singh pressed his lips together before answering. "The dead we saw were lying face up, cut open from chest to groin, their guts spread out around them. We saw the Izkop doing the same thing to dead soldiers on other parts of the field while we were shooting our way out."

Ariana looked ill, her body shaking. "Why…? Sergeant, I…I…"

"That's okay. If you can't stand dealing with them now –"

She held up one hand, palm out, her voice steadying even though she seemed to fighting off nausea. "I have to. For everyone's sake. If they'll listen. But I don't know why they - I'll call to them from here." Ariana visibly braced herself, then stood up, looking out the window, and called out some words in another language, her voice straining over glottal stops and other sounds.

The Izkop leaders ignored her, continuing their conference, then abruptly gesturing and calling out commands. With eerie synchronization the entire force of Izkop began stepping back, slowly retreating with their faces to the humans. They kept going until at least a kilometer distant, then the formations broke and the Izkop seemed to melt into the landscape.

"What the hell happened?" Goldera asked. "Not that I'm complaining, but why didn't they kill us just then?"

Singh rubbed his chin, then looked at Ariana. "Because we laughed at them?"

"Yes, but they stayed in threat posture," she responded. "And they ignored my attempts to talk to them. I'm not…oh…'the peace of the warrior before death.' *That's* what it means."

"So they'll hit us later?"

"Yes." Ariana sagged, her face in her hands. "It's a mark of respect, not a reprieve. There's no set period for the peace that I could determine."

The sergeant nodded calmly. "At least it's obvious they know we're here. Two on watch at all times," he ordered the soldiers, "the rest get to work fortifying and blockading all the windows and doors as best we can. Don't worry any more about keeping the barricading concealed from the outside. If the Izkop haven't hit us by the time we're done with that, those off-watch will rest so we'll be ready to keep two sentries on at a time all night."

"What about us?" Ariana asked.

"Look after those kids and keep them quiet, ma'am. It'd be a big help if you all also took care of meals for everyone."

The peace before death had lasted all day. Now, long after sunset, Johansen sat near one window, searching the outside for any signs of Izkop. On the other side of the room, Stein stood sentry at another window. No lights showed inside or out, and the stars and three small moons of this world provided very little illumination.

Johansen had learned that you found out a lot when sitting

silently on sentry duty at night. No human noises around, just you and the quiet broken only by the night sounds of whatever place you were in. Listening and watching, you could hear and feel the rhythm of the creatures and the land. And once you knew that rhythm, you could tell when something was disturbing it.

Of course, without the colors and noises and activity of the day to act as distractions, ghosts came at night, too. Johansen tried to ignore the phantoms brought to life by his memories, but still the ghosts sometimes appeared in the stillness of the night.

Ariana came out of the back, hesitated, then came to sit on the floor near Johansen, her back to the wall, hugging herself.

Johansen watched her for a moment before speaking. "You okay?"

She took a deep, shuddering breath. "You mean for someone expecting to die very soon?"

"Yeah." Their voices were barely murmurs, just loud enough for the other to hear.

"No. I'm not okay." Ariana clenched her eyes shut in anger. "Why? I know what's happened, but I don't know why. It's my job to try to understand the way others think. Is it too much to ask that I be allowed to understand why my husband died and why I'm going to die and why those children have to die?"

Johansen ran one hand down his weapon, concentrating on the curves and edges of it under his palm. "People always die sooner or later. Why do any of us have to die?"

"I'm not talking about philosophy."

"Neither am I." Johansen gave her a rueful smile. "I've seen a lot of people die. Most of the time, I couldn't tell you why they died. Especially I couldn't tell you why they died and not me."

She returned a curious look. "Most of the time? Meaning sometimes you could tell why they died?"

"Sure. Sometimes they died because I shot them."

After a long moment, Ariana spoke slowly. "That was a joke?"

"Yeah," Johansen said. "Soldier humor. Some of it's pretty dark, but you either joke about it or let it give you nightmares. Sometimes both."

"Greeting death with a smile?"

"Yeah. It's nuts, but it keeps us going."

She studied him, shaking her head. "You see, I never understood that greeting death with a smile phrase. What did it mean? None of the other humans here I talked to could understand it, either. They blew it off as some kind of symbolism. I thought it must be an Izkop way of thinking, embracing death under certain circumstances. But you showed it. You and the others, and none of you want to die. Now, I think maybe I understand a little. It's not about welcoming death, it's more about laughing at death to push fear aside."

"Yeah, I guess that's right. No soldiers here, huh?"

"No. We're all researchers." Ariana looked down. "What Scorse said, about soldiers being…"

"Low class creatures with limited intellect?" Johansen asked, grinning at her reaction. "That's something Sergeant Singh calls us sometimes. But only when he's unhappy with us. One of the things you learn as a soldier, though, is that everybody's got some experience, some way of thinking that might be useful. Most people, anyway. I've met a few who couldn't walk and chew gum at the same time, but only a few. You need all kinds. I've been around enough to know that everything can't be solved with firepower. Right now, I guess that's all we've got, but I wouldn't mind some other options. At least there's something we can do. I don't know what it's like for you and the other civilians."

"We're not used to any of this," Ariana said. "The danger. Taking care of the children. Scorse isn't helping at all with that, and even though Juni's okay with children I can tell he resents acting as a baby-sitter."

"Well, yeah, big shot research guy, huh? I mean, he seems okay, but that's the sort of job he figures he's supposed to pay other people to do. You said none of the kids here are yours?"

Ariana shuddered again. "No."

"That's one good thing, then."

"Yes." She stared at Johansen. "Having children at Amity was a demonstration that we were here in peace. We kept the numbers limited so it didn't appear we were settling here. It was all supposed to show that this was peaceful and not aggressive."

Johansen made a noncommittal gesture. "I guess the Izkop didn't see it that way."

"Or it somehow didn't matter to them even if they did see what we intended." Ariana clenched her fists and her jaw, the muscles standing out clearly even in the darkness. "We all thought that we understood them well enough to know if anything was wrong, and I still have no idea why they massacred everyone at Amity. Or what the mutilation after death means. One thing I do know is that the Izkop consider children to be purer of spirit than adults. It may not be a coincidence that the Izkop moved against Amity when the children left to come here for a few days, but why that would matter if they intend killing us here as well is one more thing I don't understand."

After a long silence, Johansen cleared his throat softly. "I dated a woman for quite a while once. Moved in with each other and all that. I thought everything was fine, that we understood each other, and then one day she left. Said she'd been telling me what was bothering her, and when I didn't respond it just made her more upset."

Ariana met his eyes. "But you hadn't noticed anything?"

"Nope." Johansen looked out at the darkness, not wanting to see the fear and sorrow in her. Instead his mind conjured up a vision of Maria standing at the door to their place, her face twisted with anger, yelling at him. *How could you not know? I kept telling you!* A door slammed and Johansen started with pulse pounding and weapon coming up before he realized that sound had only echoed in his memory. "We think we can understand aliens when we can't even communicate with other humans half the time."

"I suppose that's true." Ariana bit her lip. "It's our job to understand, though, just as it's your job to fight. How could the Izkop have killed so many soldiers? Your sergeant explained, but none of us really understood."

He didn't want to recall that, but the question deserved an answer. "Um, well, when you fight, you need someone watching your sides and your back, right? Usually, that someone can be a good distance off, but against a whole mob you need them right there, otherwise while you're shooting forward some others can get behind you and grab your arms and stuff." Johansen shrugged, hoping the hammering of his heart at the memories of the massacre wasn't too obvious to her. "Like Sergeant Singh said, the battalion was scattered all over the valley."

"But why were you scattered? Didn't your leaders, your commanders, know that you needed to watch each other's backs?"

"Well…there was talk the captain, our company commander, that is, was unhappy with the plan, but the colonel, he was in charge of the whole operation, was set on dropping in a wide formation," Johansen explained. "Because it was a rescue op. We could see Izkop on the hills around the valley, in lots and lots of small groups. The colonel wanted us to cover lots of territory so we'd be wherever the civilians were in the valley. If we just dropped in a tight group then some or even all the civs might be outside the group and then the Izkop could rush in and massacre them." It seemed funny now, in a sick way. "We didn't know the Izkop already had massacred the civs at Amity, and hidden themselves all over the valley. So we got massacred, too.

"We knew they were in the hills but didn't see them waiting in the valley itself. Maybe your people showed them how IR gear and stuff like that works. They figured out how to hide from it, and our leaders didn't figure they'd do that. Just a bunch of spear-chucking primitives, right? There they are, no need to look around any more, no need to deploy special battlefield recce, especially when those civs need us now! So we dropped right in as if the whole landing zone was empty. Only it wasn't. Someone wants to kill you that bad, usually there's a real strong reason. I guess I'd like to know what the reason is, too."

"They destroyed everything in Amity, you told us," she said. "That has to be a clue. Have I mentioned Prometheus?"

"Prometheus? The Titan who stole fire from the gods?"

"You know about that Prometheus?" She smiled, then looked embarrassed. "I'm sorry. I –"

"No offense taken, ma'am."

"My students call me Professor Tisrok. My friends call me Ariana. No one calls me ma'am."

He couldn't help grinning at her. "So what am I?"

"Call me Ariana. The Izkop legends have a figure I call Prometheus. But the status of the Izkop Prometheus is confusing to me. Is he a god? Or a demon? He seems to be both. The Izkop value knowledge, but also fear having their souls corrupted by accepting things stolen from the gods."

"You think maybe the Izkop decided humans were working with Prometheus?" Johansen asked.

"Maybe," she said cautiously. "But our policies should have prevented the Izkop from ever thinking that. We never gave them anything. What happened that translated into massacre? What did the Izkop think happened? If only…"

"Yeah?"

Ariana clenched her jaw again. "My professional opinions aren't popular. There's a lot of politics in academia. I believe that mythologies, religious beliefs, tell you a lot about how sentient creatures think. That's not fashionable right now. The orthodox, prevailing view in my field is that myths and religions are just window-dressing, not really fundamental to world-views and not regarded by cultures as serious explanations for how the universe works."

Johansen gave her a baffled look. "Where did anyone get that idea?"

"If everyone you work with and socialize with thinks like that, then it's very easy to believe that it's true of everyone else." Ariana sighed. "Like Juni, most of my colleagues back at Amity even argued that the Izkop aren't truly warlike, that the spears and the battle practices and everything else are just vestigial and symbolic. They look at a primitive society and see the noble savage."

"Noble savage?" Johansen shook his head, his eyes searching the darkness outside. "How does someone be noble and savage? And how does that correlate with being primitive?"

She laughed briefly, the sound filled with pain. "Those are exactly the sort of questions that I ask. Some very technological human societies have been very savage. Noble primitives seem to be something people want to believe in, like...like..."

"Hookers with hearts of gold?"

"Yes! Those are probably as rare in real life as noble savages."

"So," Johansen asked, "what do noble savages do?"

Ariana sighed, shaking her head. "I've been told by experts senior to me that the Izkop with their primitive technology are so closely connected to their world that they understand their place in the universe much better than we do."

"How exactly does that work?" Johansen asked after a long moment.

She caught the hint of mockery in his voice. "That's a question that Juni would answer with many words made up of many syllables. I don't believe the logic behind them. That's why I was posted out here, where I wouldn't bother others any more with my skepticism. Now perhaps I've been proven right, and those experts are now dead in Amity, and it hurts so bad. If only I'd been wrong." Her voice broke on the last words.

"You being wrong wouldn't have meant they were right."

She gave him a tormented look. "Perhaps there's something more I could have done. Something that could have saved everyone."

He watched the night outside for a moment being replying, glad that her presence had driven off the ghosts. "Nobody can save everybody. It's not your fault." He'd been told that, years ago. He hadn't believed it. Not really. He wondered if she would.

Ariana inhaled deeply, then fell silent, so they just sat there for a long time until she dozed off and Adowa came to relieve him on the watch. Adowa raised a questioning eyebrow at Johansen as she pointed at Ariana, but he just shook his head and gestured for quiet.

When dawn came, there were no Izkop visible. Johansen felt hope stir.

The morning dragged on with nothing moving outside except the wandering path of the cow and an occasional sighting of a wild creature in the grass or the sky. Archer nursed her comm unit but heard nothing. They checked and rechecked the barricades at the doors and larger windows. Singh moved from soldier to soldier, giving advice and calming talks, but no one said much, as if afraid too much conversation would draw the Izkop out.

Juni had been pacing back and forth most of the morning, and now peered out the window toward the cow, which mooed piteously. "I should go out. I'll get the milk, and come back. The Izkop aren't doing anything today."

Singh shook his head. "No, sir. Please stay inside."

"But it's *safe*. It's almost noon and -"

Ariana suddenly gasped. "Noon. 'The banner of the sun flaming its highest.' Sergeant, one Izkop myth says that's when heroes die."

"And they might think we're heroes? Everybody to the windows!" Singh barked at the soldiers. "Ma'am, you and the others get in with the kids. Call us if there's any sign the Izkop are trying to get in through the back."

Ariana ran toward the rear of the building, grabbing Juni as she went, but Scorse fended her off. "I'll stay out here," he growled.

Johansen took a long slow breath, his rifle resting on the sill of the window. Behind him, the door to the back room shut. Outside, a flying creature spiraled into the air from the surface of the meadow. "Something scared it," Goldera said. "They're out there."

Shouts echoed between the bluffs. The Izkop seemed to rise out of the ground a kilometer away and came forward at a steady pace, staying shoulder to shoulder as they moved. "Hold fire until I give the command!" Singh called, also kneeling at a window. "Make every shot count!"

"Hell, Sarge," Goldera commented, "with them lined up like that even Archer couldn't miss."

"Shut up," Archer snapped back at him, sounding for a moment more annoyed than scared.

As the Izkop drew closer, Johansen found himself focusing on small things. The way their hips worked as they moved, not quite like a human's would. The bright gleam of the short stabbing spears every Izkop carried. The faces which seemed curiously impassive to human eyes. The tough vegetation being crushed beneath the serried ranks of Izkop.

"Fire!"

Johansen aimed and fired as fast as he could, the solid oncoming block of Izkop an impossible-to-miss target. To his right he heard the thunderous whirr of the buzz-saw pumping out rounds, Nassar walking the stream of bullets across the formation to drop Izkop like a scythe felling reeds in long lines.

The Izkop came inside the fence, rushing toward the building, while the soldiers fired, reloaded and fired again. The entire compound seemed to be packed with Izkop, a seething mass which lapped against the building like a flood, then abruptly pulled back, retreating to the fence and continuing their withdrawal.

"Cease fire!" Another shot rang out and Singh glowered at Burgos. "Cease fire, dammit!"

"Oh, man." Goldera stared at the mounds of dead Izkop outside. "They're crazy. They just kept coming. We are so dead."

"They'll be back," Singh agreed, "but we're not dead yet."

A wild mooo echoed through the sky, followed by the appearance of the cow trotting quickly across the yard, her panic-stricken eyes huge and rolling as she dodged the piles of dead.

The soldiers simply watched it wordlessly for a long moment before Archer said something in a wondering voice. "They didn't kill the cow?"

Another long silence, then Stein spoke with great deliberation. "Maybe they like cows."

Archer grinned, too wide and too stressed for the gesture to represent real humor. "Next time they hit us, I'm going to be behind that cow."

"No. I mean it. Maybe they're like the Sarge's people."

Singh bent a severe look on Stein. "I'm a Sikh, not a Hindu."

"Oh. Right."

"Anybody hurt? No? Ammo inventory," Singh ordered.

Nassar waved toward the discarded buzz-saw. "I've got sixty-five rifle rounds left, but the machine gun's out. Now it's only good for hitting them over the head with."

"We'll probably need it for that," Adowa said. "Thirty-two rifle rounds remaining, Sarge, plus twenty for my pistol."

"I got forty," Archer reported. "Uh, no pistol," she added unnecessarily since as the comm carrier she didn't also lug a side arm.

"Thirty-one," Stein said in an apologetic voice. "And one clip for the pistol. That's twenty, right?"

"You taking time to aim again, Stein?" Goldera joked in a strained voice. "I got twenty-nine for the rifle. No pistol."

"What happened to your side arm?" Johansen demanded.

"I dunno. When we got clear of the drop ship it wasn't there. I didn't think I should go back looking for it."

"Eleven rounds rifle, twenty pistol," Burgos said, then looked away when Singh glared at her again.

"We need to exercise fire discipline," the sergeant said coldly. "Corporal?"

"Twenty-four and twenty for the pistol," Johansen said.

Singh looked out the window, his eyes calculating. "We might be able to fight off another attack before the ammo is gone. Maybe not. Then it'll be hand-to-hand."

"They got a lot more hands than we do," Adowa said. "Any chance we can get some of those spears off the bodies out there? Those have more reach than our combat knives."

'It wouldn't hurt." Singh turned his gaze back on them. "Not at night. It'd give us cover, but it'd give the Izkop a lot more. Any volunteers to go out there now?"

Johansen blew out a tired breath into the silence. "I'll go."

"Me, too," Goldera hastened to add. The others removed the barricade at the front door enough for the two to slip out, then Johansen and Goldera scuttled toward some of the dead Izkop, staying low.

Johansen grabbed some of the spears, watching carefully in case any of the Izkop were playing possum and still able to stab. He passed the spears to Goldera, who kept one eye on the fields beyond the compound. "Hey, corporal," Goldera whispered.

"Yeah?"

"You scared?"

"Damn right."

"Me, too," Goldera confessed. "If you get out of this and I don't, write my mama and tell her I did okay even though I was scared. Will you do that?"

"Sure." He picked up a final two spears. "That's two apiece for all of us. Let's get back inside."

"You got anybody you want me to tell anything if you don't make it?" Goldera asked Johansen.

Johansen didn't have to think about it. "Nah. Not anymore." Then they were squeezing inside and the door being sealed again in their wake.

Singh had them all try out the spears, which Johansen found

to be well-balanced for stabbing though far too front-heavy for throwing. Then everyone settled down again, the civilian adults once again all in the front room. "It's hard being in there with the kids," Juni complained. "They keep asking what's happening, when they're going home, can they talk to their parents. We told them to play and stay quiet."

"It's going to be a long afternoon," Singh observed. "Tell us something about the Izkop," he asked the civilian researchers.

Scorse grimaced. "I'm a planetary geologist. I never cared about them."

Juni shrugged. "I'm a planetary ecologist. I don't study one species, I study the whole system. I received my doctorate at Old Harvard under Professor Haddleton, you know. I know how everything contributes to the whole."

"Wow," Adowa commented in a non-committal tone.

That left Ariana, who gave Scorse and Juni cross looks before speaking. "I'm not an expert on them. I study mythic structures."

"That probably makes you the biggest living expert," Burgos grumbled.

Ariana winced as Singh and Johansen both pinned Burgos with glares. "That's true. What do you want to know about the Izkop?"

"We know they're farmers and herders. That was in the predrop brief." Singh gestured outward. "Tell us something about how they think. You said something about heroes before. Meeting death with smiles. What kind of heroes have the Izkop got?"

Ariana hesitated. "There's one hero they call the pass-holder. Their greatest hero. I call him Horatio, after an ancient human hero who held a bridge. The Izkop Horatio held a pass against demons who were trying to wipe out the ancestors of the Izkop. He died holding the pass. I haven't been able to figure out whether they revere him for saving their ancestors, or for dying while holding the pass. I have a feeling their admiration has at least partly to do with the fact that he died, and would be the same even if he hadn't succeeded. I mean, presumably there wouldn't be any Izkop if he'd failed, but what mattered was that he died. Or was willing to die. I think."

"Hmmm." Singh blew out a long breath, his eyes still on the outside. "This Horatio was one of the founders of their race?"

"No. He was something separate. That mattered, too. He wasn't of them but he died saving them. Does that make sense?"

"It does to me," Goldera commented. "The whole Jesus thing, right?"

"Well, yes, but Horatio wasn't the son of their God. The Izkop don't have one God. They have many gods, and each of those gods is many things. The theology is incredibly complex," Ariana continued, warming to her talk. "Each god can look like anybody or anything. Disguise, concealment, is very big in the Izkop myths and legends. Disguised gods and demons are everywhere, either looking for Izkop to reward for their deeds or trying to corrupt the Izkop with temptations."

"Like the Prometheus guy you told me about?" Johansen said.

"Prometheus." Ariana shook her head. "He's very hard to figure out. I use the name Prometheus for him because he steals the gifts of the gods and tries to give them to the Izkop, like ancient Greek myths say the Titan Prometheus stole fire from the gods and gave it to humans."

"What did the other gods do to Prometheus for stealing their secrets?" Johansen asked. "In the Greek myths didn't Prometheus get chained to a mountain?"

"Yes!" Ariana gave Johansen a happy look, clearly pleased to have found a kindred spirit. "He was chained to a mountain and a vulture ate his liver every day. Since he was immortal the liver regrew every night. But the Izkop Prometheus, if I understand it right, hasn't been punished because the gods can't catch him."

"Because he can look like anybody and anything?" Goldera asked.

"Exactly, only Prometheus, and the other gods and demons, aren't really 'he.' Each one is 'they' because they're simultaneously different sexes and no sex."

Goldera squinted at her for a moment. "This isn't a Garden of Eden type thing?"

"No, for a couple of reasons. Prometheus is always trying to give the gods' secrets to the Izkop. It's an ongoing crime or temptation, rather than some ancient act. And also because the gods can't catch and punish Prometheus. Only the Izkop can identify Prometheus. From what I've seen in their mythology, with its emphasis on disguises, the Izkop put a great deal of importance on actions, not appearance."

"Kind of the opposite of humans?" Adowa remarked dryly.

"In a way, yes. Even though humans don't look the same as them, the Izkop didn't seem bothered by that when we landed. I think it's because the Izkop always cared more about what we did than they do about our appearance. It's possible," Ariana continued in a cautious voice, "that the Izkop have as much trouble seeing emotions in each others' expressions as humans do trying to see feelings in an Izkop. We're not sure. The emphasis on actions over looks might be the result of them all naturally having what we'd call poker faces."

Nassar shook his head. "What'd the people in the valley do, then? Are you saying the Izkop are reacting to something the humans did?"

Scorse had fixed a burning gaze on Ariana, who pretended to ignore it. "I think something must have happened which made the Izkop believe that we had done something."

"They blew up everything," Archer said. "That tells us something, right? Did they think all of the human equipment had come from this Prometheus guy?"

"They couldn't have! We didn't give them anything. That was a firm rule."

"You said people showed them stuff," Adowa noted.

"Well…yes," Ariana conceded. "But there were rules. Let them see things, so they could understand they were just tools, nothing magic or accursed. And the Izkop have gradually shown more interest in our equipment. They know some human words, and the most common ones we hear are probably 'show us use it.' So we show them how we use something. They've been asking that more, from what I understand, and why would they be doing that if they thought our equipment was the property of the gods?"

"It's natural curiosity," Juni said in a low voice. "Universal survival behaviors linked to integrated conceptualization of their environment. *Not* superstition."

Ariana sighed. "If the Izkop thought our equipment was something stolen by Prometheus from the gods, if they thought we humans were working for or with Prometheus, why would they keep showing interest in the equipment? And if showing interest in the equipment is okay for them, how could that have triggered a massacre?"

"It doesn't make sense," Singh agreed.

"It doesn't make sense to *us*," Johansen said.

Burgos spoke in a flat voice. "They're going to kill us, and they've already killed a lot of people. Who cares why? All we can do is kill as many of them as we can."

Annoyed at how Burgos had dismissed Ariana, Johansen shook his head. "I'd like to know why someone or something wants to kill me, and if I can understand that maybe I can figure out how to stay alive."

"Right," Singh said. "We need every advantage we can get. It's too bad we don't know more about the Izkop."

Juni flushed and stood up abruptly, as if the comment had somehow been aimed at him. "I'm going to milk the cow. It needs it, and we need the milk."

"Juni?" Ariana stared at him. "After that attack? You're not serious."

"Of course I'm serious." He pointed toward the back room. "We need the milk. And it's obvious that the Izkop won't stop me. They haven't stopped me any other time."

"Juni –"

"Why would they hurt me? I'm not a threat to them. I'm not posturing as a threat. I've always gotten along with them. I'm an ecologist! They're close to the land. They understand living in harmony, in balance. *I* don't disrupt the balance." Juni held up the milk bucket, his face pale but determined. "I'm going out. It'll take fifteen minutes. I'll be fine."

Ariana cast a pleading look at Singh, who shook his head. "Sir, I think you'll die if you go out there."

Juni kept addressing Ariana. "The Izkop need to see some normal, routine behaviors. Something which indicates that we understand how things are interconnected. I'll show them that we are working to get the environmental imperative back in balance. That always works. Analyze the system and take corrective active. Right now they're reacting to the presence of these soldiers, this disruptive factor in the eco-system, so everything's out of balance."

"Sir," Singh said carefully, "there weren't any soldiers around when the Izkop wiped out everyone in the valley."

"And we have only your word for that, don't we? How long has the military really been here and what did *they* do? We had no problems here until soldiers came!"

Adowa had the look of someone who couldn't believe what she was hearing. "What we did was come here to try to save your butts and lost a lot of friends. No problems here? What happened to your friends and their truck? What happened to your emergency equipment?"

"There's something you're not telling us," Juni insisted, "or more likely something you don't know. I've supervised assistants. You're just…workers. No disrespect, but you have very limited perspectives. I know the big picture, and I can fit in the details. I *understand* what's happening. And that's why I know I need to stop acting as an au pair and get to work as an expert in ecological synergism!"

"By risking your life to milk a cow?" Ariana asked in despair.

"Juni, there's plenty of room for guilt in the misjudgments we all must have made, but blaming others and throwing your life away won't make up for any errors that led to this mess." She looked toward Scorse for support, but he just glowered at the floor.

Juni flushed again. "It sounds like you're judging me already. If my projections and assessments were sub-optimal, it was due to independently functioning variables whose impact on the planetary organism could not be forecast."

"Sergeant, can't you stop him?" Ariana asked.

"No, ma'am. I have no place to lock him up, no one to spare to guard him, and if I did lock him up or tie him up that'd just mean he died helpless when the Izkop overran the place." Singh looked at Juni. "Sir, I advise against this in the strongest possible terms."

"I know what I'm doing," Juni said.

"If you're determined to go out there then Goldera will go with you to the side door and bar it behind you. He'll open it only when he hears you call from the other side and confirms that there's no Izkop with you. Understand?"

"If that's required to satisfy you. I'll be back pretty quickly, and then you'll see how the Izkop react to proper non-confrontational stimuli."

An hour passed, Goldera calling out occasionally to reassure them that he was okay but that Juni had not returned. Ariana sat huddled together, her face a mask of resignation and despair, until the children raised a fuss and she had to go in to deal with them. Scorse might have been made of stone, staring silently across the room.

Finally, Singh gave Johansen permission to look for Juni. "Don't leave the building. Just do a visual recce of the yard."

Taking Adowa along, Johansen led the way to the side entry still barred shut and guarded by Goldera. "Still nothing?"

"Not a sound. Haven't heard anything except that cow mooing every once in a while."

"Okay. We open it quick and I look out. Hopefully if any Izkop are waiting we'll surprise them. If they rush us, get that door sealed even if I'm stuck on the other side. Got it?" Adowa and Goldera nodded.

Johansen took up position near the door, his weapon held at shoulder height, ready to fire. Adowa and Goldera, working together, yanked open the bars and pulled the door open fast without regard for the noise, then Johansen stepped into the opening, quivering with tension.

The yard lay silent in the afternoon light. From here, none of the Izkop bodies littering the front of the compound were visible. About a hundred meters distant in the barn, the cow stood looking back at him blankly. After carefully studying everything he could see for signs of Izkop, Johansen focused on the figure sprawled several meters from the door.

Juni's body lay face up, his abdomen torn open and entrails spread to either side, his mouth still open in a silent cry, his expression locked into incomprehension.

Adowa edged to the door and took a look. "From the way he bled, they killed him fast and quiet, then tore him open."

"How?" Goldera gasped. "I was listening. I didn't hear anything!"

Johansen pointed toward the milk bucket lying in the dirt, the soil around it wet with spilled milk. "They let him milk the cow before they killed him. They really seem to care about that animal."

"Sure wish I was that cow," Adowa muttered.

"Yeah." Stepping back inside, Johansen gestured to the others. "Seal it."

"We going to leave him out there?"

Johansen hesitated. "There's no place to put him in here. We'll bury him proper if we get the chance later."

"More likely we'll be lying out here with him," Adowa said. "I sure hope I'm dead when they cut me open." She gave Johansen a sharp look. "Neither of you guys are going to make any comments about Old Harvard?"

Johansen looked at the dead man and shook his head. "Nah. Overkill."

"Yeah," Goldera agreed.

Ariana took the news with a sad nod.

Scorse finally spoke once more. "I'll use one of those spears next time they attack. I'll stay here and fight."

All Ariana did was nod again. "Sergeant, I'd appreciate help with getting the meal."

"Johansen. You and Archer. Eat while you're helping so you can stand watch while the rest of us eat."

The Izkop came in the night this time, their numbers undiminished, filling the yard as the soldiers emptied their rifles and pulled out their pistols, the piles of dead Izkop forming ramps in front of the windows so that some Izkop came running and hurling themselves inside while others smashed through the front entry. The soldiers' weapons had little muzzle flash, providing just enough light to see the masses of Izkop as the soldiers fired, then the last pistol was empty and they fought in the dark, stabbing with knife and spear at smaller figures, Johansen being forced backwards toward the rear of the room and praying that he wouldn't accidentally spit either Archer or Goldera. He could hear Scorse over by Stein, the civilian yelling obscenities as he fought with an Izkop spear. Burgos also shouted from her post near the door until her voice fell silent.

Pain burned as a spear went into his thigh. Johansen thrust back, despairing as the bodies pushed forward shouting in the Izkop language, then as he made another stab Johansen realized the pressure had lessened, that the movement of the enemy had changed. The area in front of him held only a couple of Izkop, then none as the aliens fell back through the door and windows again, leaving the humans alone in the building.

There was a moment of strange almost-silence then, the only noises the harsh breathing of the soldiers trying to catch their breath and the faint sounds of the mass of Izkop fading into the night. Sergeant Singh spoke first. "I'm moving to the door. I'm there. All the Izkop here seem dead. Burgos is on the threshold. She's got a dozen spears in her. No pulse. Everybody else report."

"Johansen here," he said, trying to keep his voice steady. "Got a bad wound in one thigh. Everything else seems minor."

"Adowa. Got one or two deep cuts in my right arm and lots of minor stuff."

"Nassar. Just small stuff. I'll live."

"Goldera. Small cuts. Except I think maybe I lost a finger. Oh, man, I lost two."

After a pause, Singh called out. "Stein. You still with us?"

The answer came from Nassar. "Here he is by the window. Oh, hell. Stein's dead, Sarge. So's that civ, Scorse."

"Damn. Archer? Archer?"

No answer.

"We need to find Archer, people," Singh ordered. "Adowa, Johansen, Goldera, you three patch each other up enough to stop major bleeding. Nassar, look for Archer now unless the other three need first aid help. I'll keep an eye on the outside."

They fumbled in the darkness, cursing, until Singh told them to use hand lights. "The Izkop know we're here. Use enough light to take care of bad wounds and find Archer. She must be buried under some of the dead Izkop. And make sure all of those Izkop in here *are* dead."

Half an hour later, med patches melding into their skin to seal off the worst injuries and stop bleeding, the five remaining soldiers halted their search of the building. "She's gone, Sarge," Nassar said. "Archer's not here. They took her."

"The comm unit is gone, too," Adowa reported. "Why'd they take Archer?"

Goldera replied in a bone-weary voice. "Why not ask why they stopped and left? We were all dead in another minute or two. Why'd they stop?"

No one tried to answer that. Johansen sagged against a table, looking out into the darkness, feeling no hope, no curiosity, just tiredness and a resigned sort of fear.

An inside door opened, spilling pale radiance across the front room littered with dead. Ariana stood in the doorway, her breath catching at the sight of them still standing. "The children are scared. They heard all the fighting. What do I tell them?"

"Damned if I know, ma'am," Singh said. "I guess all you can tell them is that we're still here."

"That's a lot," she finally replied. "They still believe in heroes."

Johansen felt himself straightening up at her words, standing a little taller despite his weariness and injuries, and noticed the others doing the same.

After Ariana had closed the door again, Nassar gusted a single soft and sardonic laugh. "If we got to die anyway, it's nice to know someone appreciates it."

Sergeant Singh nodded, his expression impossible to make out in the dark. "We got one more fight left in us. Two-hour sentry duty, one soldier on at a time so the others can rest."

"You don't think they'll come again tonight, Sarge?" Goldera asked.

"I still don't know what they'll do, let alone why they're doing it. All we can do is protect those kids for one more night, and hope that effort of ours somehow matters to the Iskop when they've got the kids at their mercy."

Johansen had the watch when the sky began paling with dawn's light. He sat on the floor, leaning against the wall next to the window, looking outward, an Izkop spear in one hand, as the growing daylight began turning the vague, gray shapes of night into clear objects with color and meaning. The med patch kept his thigh numb, and while that served as a reminder of the wound it covered it also meant that when just sitting here he could pretend it wasn't a bad injury. Sitting quietly felt right anyway. In that strange stillness that dawn always held, there might have been nothing else living on the entire planet except for themselves and the distant shape of one of the local flying predators wheeling across the sky.

Silence and stillness. The right and left hands of death, someone had called them. She had died, too, on a planet far distant, gone cold and quiet like the mounds of Izkop here lying forlorn in the growing light. He thought about other dawns to come, without him around anymore. The idea felt impossible, and strange, even after all he had seen.

Archer was out there somewhere, but he tried not to think of that, except to wish that she got it like Juni had, a quick death before any mutilation.

He heard soft sounds behind and looked quickly to see that Ariana had come out of the back. She seemed to be emotionally used up and physically exhausted from dealing with the children, but that really shouldn't matter much longer. "Mornin'," Johansen whispered to her, pain stabbing through the numbness inside him as he thought about Ariana dying, too. One more person he couldn't save.

She reached the wall and leaned next to him, her eyes on his face. "Good morning. Are they out there?"

"I expect. Can't see any of them, of course."

Rising up a bit, she looked out as well, their shoulders touching for a moment before Ariana slumped back again. "I thought soldiers had all sorts of special equipment built into their bodies, to let you see in the dark and do other things."

"No, that's just in stories," Johansen said. "In real life, they kept finding out that implanting gear into people, biomechanicals and stuff, created a huge Achilles Heel. Anything like that could be hacked or intruded or jammed. One good hack could take out an entire force.

Eventually, they decided the only firewall good enough was maintaining physical separation between human and equipment."

She actually smiled slightly. "No secret superpowers to save the day?"

"Nope. Just the same old, same old as back at Troy." Johansen tapped his spear.

"Does that make me Cassandra?" Ariana sighed. "What were you thinking about before I came out here?"

He hesitated before answering. "I was thinking how strange it is to know that this is the last sunrise I'll ever see. I mean, there's always a chance any sunrise will be your last, but this time it's certain. Kind of a weird feeling. At least it's a pretty sunrise."

"Yes, it is. Are you sorry you came here?"

"Well, yeah." Johansen glanced at her. "Not that we came to this spot. We would have died anyway, and at least coming here meant a chance for you and the kids. But this planet I could have done without."

Ariana stared at the bodies of Burgos, Stein and Scorse against the far wall as if unable to believe that they were real. "I thought they'd last the longest. Scorse, I mean, and that woman soldier."

"Burgos?" Johansen shook his head. "She was pretty certain to die early on. After the massacre in the valley and watching Ramada gutted, all Burgos cared about was killing Izkop. Your Scorse seemed to be the same way."

"But if they wanted to keep killing –"

"I said that was all they cared about. They didn't care about living any more, just killing. People who get like that don't tend to last too long, because self-preservation just doesn't occur to them."

She gave Johansen a quizzical look. "But you want to kill Izkop, too, and you told me that you don't expect to live."

"No, but you see I only want to kill Izkop so I have a chance to live." Somehow Johansen mustered a small smile as he watched the sun rising over the bluffs. "Get me out of here in one piece and I'd be happy never to kill another Izkop. But not Burgos and Scorse. They'd have jumped right back in."

"But don't you want revenge? For all of your friends killed back at Amity?"

He shook his head. "Revenge never brought back anyone. It's just something those still alive do for themselves. I could kill every Izkop on this planet and it wouldn't give me back a single friend. I know that. So did Burgos, but she didn't care. I figure my friends would want me to go on living. To try to, anyway. That's what I'd want for them if I was the one dying."

"What about the big one? He seemed so calm, so steady."

"Stein?" Johansen exhaled heavily. "Yeah. He wasn't the brightest star in the sky, but he was loyal. He was fighting alongside Scorse, so he wouldn't leave him, wouldn't fall back alone. That wouldn't even have occurred to Stein."

Ariana nodded, her head lowered. "And Juni."

"Don't blame yourself for that. Juni was stupid." Out of the corner of his eye, Johansen could see Ariana's head come up, tears lining her face. "We told him not to go out there. He went anyway. Most of the time in life, stupid just gets you in trouble. In a combat situation, stupid gets you dead. I'm sorry," he added, because he was. "Juni seemed like a decent guy. And it's not like he was trying to run out on us. He was trying to do something he thought was important. He just thought he knew more than he did. People who think they know all the answers seem to often end up killing themselves or other people in one way or another."

She didn't reply, just crying as she looked toward the door leading to the back room. "Listen," Johansen said as gently as he could, "when they get done with us, they'll break down that door. You just stand there and you beg, you hear me? You can't fight, so plead with them. Beg for the lives of the kids. Not for you, for them. Sometimes that makes a difference. Tell them whatever humans did, or whatever the Izkop think we did, it wasn't the fault of the kids."

Ariana nodded. "You'll be dead if they get to that door?"

"Yeah. They won't get to it before then. I'm really sorry."

"Don't be sorry. Thanks for being Horatio."

"I'm no hero, but you're welcome. I've got to admit, I don't understand why you civilians come to places like this."

She actually smiled slightly. "We come to try to learn more about others and about ourselves. Humans, that is. There's plenty of civilians who wouldn't understand why you're here. Guarding that door even though it's hopeless. You don't understand why we do what we do, and we don't understand why you do what you do, and neither group of us understands why the Izkop are doing what they are doing."

"I hope they at least have a good reason," Johansen said dryly. "As long as I'm going to die because of it." Shapes appeared in the distance, coming around one of the bluffs. "Sarge!"

Singh was up at his own window in a matter of seconds as the rest of the surviving soldiers also jerked awake and scrambled into position. "What've we got?"

"A small group," Johansen reported, squinting to try to make out details. "Maybe ten Izkop, coming down the bluff to the right. They're carrying something."

"Only a dozen?" Singh brought up his field glasses, studying the group as it slowly came closer, walking at a deliberate pace toward the building. "They've got Archer."

"She's still alive?" Nassar cried.

"Maybe." Singh's mouth worked as he kept the field glasses on the group, then he spat to one side. "I can't tell. They're carrying her. She's upright, but not walking herself." The sergeant lowered the field glasses and slid toward Johansen, keeping low. He spoke softly. "If she is still alive, they might torture her to death in front of us. Be ready to help hold back the others if that happens."

"I wish we could just charge out and get it over with," Johansen growled, anger warring with despair within him. "But we still got the kids back there."

Singh let out a sigh. "Right. We secure this building as long as we can, corporal."

The sergeant returned to his own window, the other soldiers staying at their own posts. As the small group of Izkop came closer, Johansen could see that Archer was limp and being supported by several of the Izkop. Even though Archer was fairly small, the Izkops' own small stature meant that her feet dragged and bumped over the ground as the group approached.

Ariana was right next to him again, her breathing ragged as she also looked at the approaching group. "What's going on?"

"I was hoping you had some idea," Johansen said. Closer still, the light of dawn growing, they could see rips in Archer's battle fatigues and wide smears of blood. Her head lolled down so they couldn't see her face, but Johansen thought he saw raw wounds down the sides of her neck.

"I've never seen anything like this," Ariana said. "It's clearly a procession. That one in the lead, the old Izkop, he's wearing decorations that indicate very high rank."

The small group of Izkop stopped at the gate, then came on another couple of meters with a slow gait that seemed ceremonial to Johansen. Archer's head came up for a moment as if that gesture took all of her strength, then flopped down once more.

"She is alive!" Adowa shouted, beginning to rise from her crouch near the door.

"Hold position," Singh ordered, his voice as dark and commanding as that of a stern god. Goldera let out a curse that sounded like a sob, and Adowa settled back onto her knees, her face drawn.

The old Izkop in the lead gestured to the others to halt and then spread his arms wide, chanting.

"What's he saying?" Nassar demanded.

Ariana listened, her expression intent. "Something about…that god I called Horatio."

"They think Archer is Horatio?"

"No. It's more like his spirit, or example. I'm not sure what the words actually mean." She looked confused now. "The Izkop… proved…their…purity? But so did…Archer. I think that's a reference to Archer and…her people. I'm sorry, but he's using the ceremonial language which is even harder to understand than the common speech." Ariana shook her head. "I think he's referring to all of you. The others who came among the…demons. No, thieves. Both, maybe. In the valley. Oh, no, they're talking about us. The civilians. Something belonging to gods. False…hands? No. Offerings. False offerings. Corruption. I think that refers to spiritual, not physical corruption. Something about that demon god I call Prometheus. Denial. Test. Honor. Test. Strength. True…protectors? Of Izkop. Of the gods."

The six Izkop carrying Archer lowered her to the ground, face up, then held up their spears in salute before raising them again, points down, ready to strike. "No," Adowa got out in a strangled whisper.

But when the Izkop slammed their spears into the dirt, they did so on either side of Archer. The leader raised his hands, calling out in a voice that echoed across the landscape.

Johansen had sudden trouble breathing as thousands of Izkop rose up from the surrounding terrain, standing silently, spears by their sides. His hands slid along the shaft of his own spear, suddenly slick with sweat. He heard a low murmuring sound and realized that Sergeant Singh was praying, perhaps a final benediction before death.

"You put on your damned show, now just do it and get it over with," Nassar got out between gritted teeth as the Izkop stood silently.

Then the leader raised his hands once more, shouting another command. Just as the first small group had, the masses of Izkop raised their spears, holding them high canted toward the building, then shouted as one before reversing the weapons and driving them point first into the ground like those already planted around Archer.

A third command from the leader, and all of the Izkop began moving back, leaving their spear shafts standing like a low forest bare of branches and leaves. The long ranks of Izkop all around as well as the small group with the leader marched steadily away, leaving Archer lying amid the spears thrust into the dirt around her.

The Izkop had almost vanished over the surrounding ridges when Singh shook his head like someone coming out of a dream. "Nassar, you and Goldera go out there and get Archer."

Holding his spear as if that could still help cover the others, Johansen watched Nassar and Goldera hastily shove aside the bodies blocking the doorway, then trot quickly to Archer. Nassar knelt and examined her while Goldera stood on guard. "She's been cut up quite a bit," Nassar called back to the others. "Not deep wounds. Like she was sliced with knives. Can't tell if there's any internal injuries but I can't spot any broken bones. Hey, Archer's still got the comm unit."

"What?" Singh demanded.

"Yeah. She's holding the damned comm unit in both arms. Won't let go."

"Let her hold on to it. Just bring her in."

They got her inside, where Ariana rushed to help treat Archer. Johansen saw that Archer's face was almost unmarked except for long cuts down each cheek and on her temples leading down toward her eyes but stopping short. "Get her awake," Singh ordered. "We have to know what happened and what all of that meant."

One of the injections from the first aid kit did the trick. Archer's eyes shot open and her mouth trembled as she looked from side to side. "Crazy," she gasped.

"No," Singh assured her. "You're back. The Izkop brought you back. Why?"

"They...what?"

Adowa leaned in closer. "Hey, princess, will you let go of the damned comm unit so we can work on your arms and chest?" she demanded.

"Huh? That really you, Addy?" Archer seemed incapable of unclasping her hands, but with the help of Adowa managed to release the comm unit. She looked around again, her eyes tearing up. "What the hell?"

"You're s–" The sergeant broke off the word 'safe,' apparently realizing how absurd it would be to say that. "You're okay. Tell us what happened," Singh said, his voice more gentle but still commanding.

"What…" Archer closed her eyes, her mouth slack for a moment, then rallied. "I was…fighting and something hit…my head. Woke up, being carried –" Her voice rasped to a halt.

"Water," Singh ordered, waiting until Archer had drained a cup before speaking again. "Then what?"

"Uh…" Archer seemed unaware of the others working on her many minor injures, instead staring up at the ceiling as if seeing recent events there. "Camp of some kind. Thousands of Izkop. Tens of thousands. Some held me." She looked over to one side. "Comm unit. I still had it. Some Izkop…wanted it. Kept…*asking*. 'Give.' Wouldn't give it to him. Said no. Hell, no." Her eyes rolled back to Singh. "My job. You said hang onto Aimee."

"That's your job," the sergeant agreed. "Aimee's fine," he added to reassure Archer. "Doesn't look damaged at all. What happened next?"

"They tried to take it. Kept pulling. I…wouldn't let them. Others came up and asked. I told them all no. No way." Archer swallowed. "They…cut me…hurt…but figured they'd…kill me anyway. I wouldn't let go."

"That's all?"

"No. Some other Izkop…" Archer struggled for words. "Told me they wanted me to…to…show them how to use it. Kept saying that. 'Show us use it,' over and over. I said *no*. No frickin' way. They…uh…" She paused again, looking even paler. "Gonna kill me, they said, held spears. Hurt me real bad…if I didn't. Cut me more. Face. Other places."

"Did you show them then?" Singh asked, his voice calm and steady.

"No." Archer managed a ghastly grin. "Told them…go screw yourselves. Why not? Kill me anyway…right? Maybe make them mad, they'd…kill me quick."

Singh looked at Ariana, who shook her head in bafflement. "What happened then, Archer?"

"Uh…" Archer tried to focus on him again. "They kept trying to take Aimee. I wouldn't let go. 'Show us use it.' They kept yelling that. 'Show us use it.' I kept yelling no. Go to hell. Go ahead. Kill me. Screw all of you. No show, you bastards. You'll have to… to kill me if you want it. Over my frickin' dead body." Her voice rose slightly, gaining force, a shadow of the screams she must have thrown at her captors.

Nassar appeared baffled. "Thousands of Izkop and they couldn't take that comm unit from her?"

"They could have if they wanted to," Ariana said. "Easily enough. It must have been a ritual."

"A ritual?" Singh asked.

"Yes. They keep asking her something, and she keeps saying no, and they ask her and seem like they're trying to take it, to force her, but as long as she keeps saying no, keeps fighting them to hold it, they don't kill her and they don't actually tear it out of her hands. They hurt her, but the wounds all seem superficial. Painful, but nothing that would kill her or maim her."

"You're saying that Archer did something right?" Johansen asked.

"But what?" Adowa demanded. "What did she do?"

Singh looked at Ariana. "Show us use it?"

"That's got to be the key," she agreed. "That and Archer's refusal to give it up." Ariana sat looking at Archer. "Actions. Not words. What mattered with Horatio was what he did. What matters with Prometheus, how they identify Prometheus, is what he does. Test. That's what the old Izkop meant. The ritual was a test. To see if she was aligned with the gods, or with Prometheus."

"I don't get it," Nassar said. "If the Izkop are judging us by what we do, then why didn't they run us down after we got out of the valley? That wasn't what Horatio did. Why didn't the Izkop kill us when we ran?"

Something clicked in Johansen's head. "We happened to head this way by chance. And you kept us going toward here, Sarge. The right way. The Izkop nailed anyone who tried escaping in other directions. Maybe to the Izkop it looked like we were going to make sure we died defending others, like Horatio."

"That open path," Goldera said. "After we got here and I scouted around and the way south looked wide open? They gave us a chance to keep running, to see if we'd do it."

"Damn." Singh's eyes narrowed. "Yeah. Like you said then, Johansen, too easy. They wanted to see if we'd keep running, or if we'd dig in and defend the civs. If we'd headed south they would have cut us up right then and there."

Adowa shook her head. "So we did the hero thing. Archer did the hero thing. The Izkop think that's cool. But the rest of the battalion…what the hell did they do wrong? They didn't even get a chance to head this way."

"Prometheus," Ariana murmured. "Legions of demons."

"What?" Singh asked.

She met the sergeant's eyes, her own eyes so wide with a dawning realization that Ariana looked like some tragic cartoon figure. "The Izkop believe that you know good and evil by their actions. They tested Archer, and they've been testing humans without our realizing it, because we thought we were supposed to the ones observing and evaluating them. Every time the Izkop asked a human to show them something it was a test. It wasn't curiosity, every time it was a *test* to evaluate our actions. Despite our explanations, the Izkop must still think our equipment was something from the gods, and every time we showed them how to do something we failed a test. Bit by bit we kept showing them more as they kept testing us, until someone in Amity must have crossed a line, shown the Izkop whatever was necessary to convince the Izkop that we were aspects of Prometheus, or working for Prometheus. That's why they're cutting open the bodies! To release the spirit inside and reveal the true nature of it to the gods in the sky for their judgment! Why didn't I understand that before?"

Singh watched her, his expression grim. "Because you were thinking of physical things being stolen, or scientific concepts. Not something as simple and everyday to us as how to use the stuff we carry around. They decided you civilians were working against the gods, trying to corrupt the Izkop."

"Yes." Ariana's voice had sunken to a whisper. "The Izkop destroyed everything we'd brought in order to…save their souls. And using that same equipment to attack you…the hand of the demon turned against it. There's a myth about that. When you soldiers landed at the valley it looked to the Izkop like you were there to defend the other humans, us, the agents of Prometheus. After all, we'd called you, hadn't we? You were coming in to seize the secrets of the gods again. That made you demons, too. To the Izkop, it must have looked like Armageddon."

"An army of demons from the sky," Goldera said. "Yeah. No wonder they fought like crazy."

"But they had to present a chance for some of you soldiers to prove you were not demons, but agents of the gods. Hiding among the demons, just like demons hide among the gods. They left us alive here to see if any of you would come to aid others rather than try to steal back the secrets of the gods. It wasn't the adults here that mattered, it was the innocents, the children. When you headed this way, toward the children, it seemed your particular group might be working for the gods. And then you acted like heroes of the Izkop, laughing in the face of death and fighting to protect the children. You didn't waver when they attacked. So they captured one of you for a last test, the most important test, to see how that one soldier would act. And Archer didn't act like Prometheus at all. She refused to give any secrets away. She defended the gods' secrets and showed a willingness to die in that defense. The Izkop have decided that you soldiers, your small group, are agents of the gods. I think that's right. It's only a guess, but it fits what happened."

Adowa leaned wearily against one wall. "So what happens if you're right? Are they still going to kill us?"

"You didn't understand what they just did? I've only heard it described, but now that I know what the Izkop must have been thinking I'm certain that I'm correct. That ceremony where they saluted you and then left their spears. The Izkop surrendered to you."

It took Johansen a moment to realize that his jaw had fallen open.

Singh managed to speak first. "They...surrendered to us?"

"Yes, sergeant."

"Wait a minute," Nassar demanded. "We *won*?"

"That's right. Or rather, the defenders of the gods won. But that's you, so to us it's the same thing. I'm using the human term surrender, but I think the Izkop would call it 'acknowledging superiority in this struggle.' They won't take orders from you, but they accepted you as the victors. The moral victors, that is, because you're on the right side. The...fight...is over."

"Well, hell," Singh commented. He looked toward the bodies in the room, then out in the yard and back in the direction of the valley. "I sure wish someone had figured out some of this a little earlier. It would have saved a lot of humans, and a lot of Izkop."

"We couldn't," Ariana said. "We didn't share the right mental or cultural references with them. It wasn't until I saw you, talked with you and saw what you did, that I began to understand part of how the Izkop were thinking."

"And civilian researchers wouldn't call in soldiers until hell had already broken out," Johansen said, "because how could we know something they didn't?"

"Yes." Ariana nodded to him, seeming drained of all emotion now. "If this planet had been a university campus or a research lab, full of people who thought like we did, then everything would have been fine."

Johansen shook his head. "No. The Izkop did the same thing. Instead of really trying to figure out humans, they plugged all of us into their own mythology. After all the humans and Izkop that have died, the Izkop still don't know why you civilians or we soldiers really came here, or why we did what we did. They just think they do."

Sergeant Singh sat down heavily. "What do I always tell you guys? Mistakes cost lives. Helluva big price, though."

"All of those soldiers dead, and it was our fault," Ariana said.

"Even if it was, you paid an awful price, too. Some victory. But at least we're still alive." Singh gestured to Adowa. "Pass me that comm unit. Let's see how close the cavalry is, or if it's even shown up yet."

Goldera laughed, giddy with relief. "They're going to come charging in to save us, and you'll get to say, 'they already surrendered to me.' What do you think the general will do then?"

"Try to take credit for it," Adowa said. Outside, the cow mooed forlornly. "Why the hell didn't they kill that cow?"

"I have no idea," Ariana said. "But we'd better not kill it ourselves."

"Damn right. Anybody who wants that cow," Adowa replied, "is going to have to go through me."

Adowa and Singh started checking the comm unit for damage while Goldera and Nassar sat together, grinning and talking. Later they'd be depressed, later the extent of their losses would sink in, how many friends and companions had died, later the stresses of the last few days would haunt their nights, and they'd need everything the shrinks and the docs could provide, but for now that was forgotten in the joy of unlooked-for survival. Archer lay asleep under the influence of the meds, the visible parts of her body almost covered with strips of heal-tape.

Ariana looked at Johansen. "There'll be other sunrises for you to see."

"Yeah, I guess so. You going to be okay?"

"Someday. Like you said, my husband would want me to go on."

"What was his name?" Johansen asked.

"Eric."

"If you, uh, want to talk about it, about him, I'll listen. Sometimes talking helps. When you're ready for that."

"Thanks. I'd appreciate help with the children if you can manage that, too. You're a good man, Horatio." Ariana bowed her head into her knees as if trying to shut out everything for a little while.

Johansen moved his head enough to watch the sun rising higher. An amazing thing, seeing the sun rise. It didn't help you understand anything, but it made you believe in all sorts of things again.

AUTHOR'S NOTE
SWORDS AND SADDLES

One of the authors I enjoy reading is H. Beam Piper. Stories like his Lord Kalvan novel and those set in Paratime or among the star-faring Federation are clean and exciting tales, although a bit dated now in social and technological terms. One day I realized that very few science fiction stories are set in Kansas. I also realized that very few science fiction stories feature the US Cavalry. What would H. Beam Piper have done to fix that? He would write something like *Swords and Saddles*. And, yes, all of the details about the US Cavalry are historically accurate, as is the landscape of that part of Kansas, because this story first appeared in *Analog* magazine and Stan Schmidt insists that the big things and the small things alike in a science fiction story are correct.

SWORDS AND SADDLES

A long column of soldiers and horses moved across the rolling landscape, an intense thunderstorm pummeling them. At the head of the column walked Captain Ulysses Benton, on foot and leading his mount through the tempest like the rest of the cavalry company, peering ahead into the murk to be sure of his way. Civilians, who only saw cavalry on the Fourth of July when it paraded in dress uniforms while the band played, thought of horse cavalry as a romantic way of life. Captain Benton knew better, as did all of the troopers walking in column behind him.

The real cavalry was this, trudging through the endless prairie, mud sucking at your boots, grass slippery underfoot, your feet aching from the march, sheets of water being thrown on you from a leaden sky while gusts of wind tried to knock you from your feet and forced water through every seam and opening so that no portion of you remained dry, tugging on the lead of a horse just as weary and worn-out as you were, the horse occasionally snapping at you in its misery and irritation or jerking its head with devilish timing so the tug of the reins would threaten to topple you into the mud, your stomach almost empty since there'd been no way to make a meal, and your last seven warm meals had only been bacon and beans, but this day there wouldn't even be that, nothing but soggy hardtack since no fire could be lit under these conditions.

And all for the princely sum of thirteen dollars a month for the privates. It had been sixteen dollars a month, but Congress had cut military pay in this year of 1870.

In the middle of column, the four supply wagons jolted and jumped over the uneven ground, riding light now that most of the provisions they had carried had been used up. Two more days, Benton thought. The company of cavalry would be back at Fort Harker in two more days. The only small mercy was that he and his men all wore the new broad-brimmed black slouch hats instead of the old forage caps which wouldn't have provided any real protection from the rain.

Lightning suddenly erupted around them like an artillery barrage targeted on the column, momentarily lighting the world so brightly that men flinched and closed their eyes against the flares. Benton's foot came down hard, the way it would when walking down steps and misjudging the distance to the next step. He staggered, staying up only thanks to the fact that he had the reins wrapped around one hand, and getting another attempted nip from his ornery mount as the tired horse protested being used as a support.

Hearing some muttered curses, Benton blinked against the renewed darkness, locating Sergeant Tyndall. "Are you okay, sergeant?"

"Yes, sir, cap'n, except for being cold, tired, wet and miserable, begging your pardon, sir."

"'If you want to see a good time, join the cavalry,'" Benton quoted the recruiting motto.

"That's right, sir. It's bad enough out here in October. I hate to think of campaigning on the plains again come winter. And then that lightning, like we were back fighting Johnny Reb again. But just then I thought maybe we'd stumbled across a prairie dog town."

"Did you miss a step, too?"

"Yes, sir. I wondered if the dogs had torn up the ground, but I can't see none of their burrows, and we couldn't not see them even in this mess."

They plodded onward, men and beasts enduring the storm because they had no other choice. In a small mercy, the storm began lifting before sunset, and by the time dark came on the clouds had split to reveal the innumerable stars above. Benton walked among his soldiers after the company had halted for the night, ensuring they had taken what care of their mounts they could in these conditions, with everyone and everything soaked to the skin. There was little he and Sergeant Tyndall could do but reassure the men that another couple of days would see them back in Fort Harker.

Lieutenant Garret, who had been walking with the rear of the column behind the supply wagons, straightened to attention and gave a precise salute. "I've had what dry hardtack remains distributed to the men, captain."

"You found some? Well done." Benton rubbed his forehead, feeling exhausted but knowing that like everyone else he'd be sleeping in soggy clothing on wet ground. At that, he was better off than the enlisted men, because his uniform was of decent quality and cut, while they were still forced to wear left-over uniforms hastily and cheaply manufactured for the Civil War since the War Department had no intention of buying new enlisted uniforms until every old one had worn out.

For that matter, he should have an experienced first lieutenant in the company as well as a brand new second lieutenant, but Lieutenant Randall had died of cholera four months ago and the slow-turning wheels of the War Department had yet to produce a replacement. Fortunately, Randall must have contracted the ailment off the post, because no one else had fallen ill with it. "You've done well out here, lieutenant. Very well for a newly commissioned officer on his first field maneuvers."

Garret seemed to lose a little of his own fatigue at the words. "Thank you, sir. At one point I thought I'd literally lost my balance today."

"What's that?" Benton frowned at him. "Was it when the lightning hit?"

"Yes, sir. The ground wasn't quite where I thought it would be. The men around me and my horse all stumbled, too. It was very odd."

Benton's frown deepened. "It appears many of us experienced that, lieutenant, the lay of the ground being different in small ways than it had been a moment before. Did an earthquake strike, do you think?"

Garret looked around as if seeking evidence of such an event. "I didn't think Kansas was earthquake country, sir."

"I don't know about Kansas, but there were those earthquakes sixty or seventy years ago in Missouri. They still talk about them. One of them supposedly made the Mississippi River run backwards for a short time." Benton shook his head. "Well, if it was an earthquake it didn't last long or do any damage we know of aside from minor adjustments to the prairie. Get what sleep you can tonight, lieutenant. The horses are nearly spent. We'll have to walk all day tomorrow at an easy pace to let them recover."

"Yes, sir."

The next day dawned clear and crisp. Benton stood up, wincing from the body aches inspired by sleeping on the wet ground.

"Good morning, cap'n," Sergeant Tyndall declared, offering a steaming cup.

"Coffee? How'd you get a fire going, sergeant?"

"An old Indian trick, sir."

Benton couldn't help smiling as he took the coffee. "Lieutenant Garret, I should inform you that any time Sergeant Tyndall accomplishes some remarkable feat he attributes his success to an old Indian trick."

Garret smiled despite the fatigue still shadowing his young face. "You must have known a lot of old Indians, sergeant."

"Yes, sir, lieutenant," Tyndall agreed before searching the horizon and pointing. "Look there, cap'n. Those elevations. Right where they should be. We didn't lose our way at all yesterday afternoon." He squinted. "Looks like something's up on one of them, though."

Benton pulled out his field glasses and focused them on the higher ground. One was crowned by a squat tower he didn't recall seeing before. "What do you make of that, lieutenant?"

Garret studied the view for a while. "It appears ruined to me, sir, as if it were taller once. You see those blocks of stone to one side?"

"That explains it. It's not ruined, lieutenant. It wasn't there the last time we came this way. Someone must be building a tower up there and the stone hasn't fallen, it just hasn't been set in place yet."

"Maybe Colonel Custer had the 7th build a monument to him, cap'n," Tyndall suggested, deadpan.

Tyndall, like many cavalrymen, didn't have a high opinion of Colonel Custer. Neither, for that matter, did Benton, but he couldn't openly agree with an enlisted man on the subject. So he confined himself to addressing exactly what Tyndall had proposed. "The 7th Cavalry went through here in May, sergeant. I think we would have noticed something like that before now."

Less than an hour later the column was under way again, clothing, horses and men drying under the warmth of the rising sun and with the assistance of a brisk breeze. They walked their horses through increasingly familiar flat stretches and across rolling hills and vales, stopping at the upper reaches of the Little Arkansas River in the middle of the day to water horses and men.

Tyndall cast a puzzled glance around as they led their horses through the river, the column having to shift northwards as several men and horses unexpectedly floundered into deeper water. "Sir, the ford's not the same. It should be down there a little ways."

"Lieutenant Garret and I wondered if we'd experienced an

earthquake during the storm," Benton commented. "Perhaps that changed the ford, sergeant."

"Could be, sir." But Tyndall kept throwing suspicious glances at the river until it was out of sight.

In the late afternoon they came up out of a long, shallow gulley, following a well-known route, though oddly lacking in any signs that other horses or wagons had passed this way for a long time. "Cap'n?" Sergeant Tyndall was looking up and to the side, a baffled expression on his face.

Benton followed the sergeant's gaze, blinked in disbelief, then looked again. "Where did that come from?" A low elevation over-looked the plains here, not so much a hill as a high point with gentle slopes in all directions. He had ridden past this area at least a dozen times that Benton could recall, and the ground had never shown anything but the long grasses of the prairie, a few outcrops of weathered sandstone, and crossing it at an angle the ruts from an old northern section of the Santa Fe Trail. Now something else stood there, what seemed to be the sprawling ruins of a fortress which had once covered at least fifty acres, if not more.

Tyndall was rubbing his eyes and then staring at the ruins. "You see it, too, sir? Cap'n, I figure we're twelve or thirteen miles south-south-east of the fort, and that ain't never been here. How the hell could someone have thrown that up since we came past last time?"

"I don't know." Benton held up one hand. "Column halt! Lieu-tenant Garret, remain here with the company while the sergeant and I go examine that…whatever it is."

Handing off their horses' reins to the bugler, Benton and the sergeant found the walk to the edges of the ruins was unexpectedly difficult, as the ground close to the walls proved to be studded with fragments of partially-buried sandstone blocks. As they neared a broken section of the wall, Tyndall let out a low whistle. "Look at them rocks. Someone went to a whole lot of trouble building this place, cap'n."

Someone had, Benton thought, studying the size and number of the sandstone blocks which had been set into thick walls which might have risen a dozen feet when whole. He hoisted himself through a gap in the remains of the wall, Tyndall following.

Picking their way along streets buried by blowing dirt, the tall prairie grass growing everywhere the dirt had found lodgment, they discovered badly-eroded and fallen-in buildings covering the area inside the wall. The ever-present Kansas wind blew through the ruins, sighing as it swayed the prairie grass and caressed the ancient sandstone. At the end of the street they were following, Benton saw a massive structure whose walls still seemed mostly intact, though like all the other buildings the roof had long ago collapsed. Walking up a short grass-covered slope which had once been a broad staircase, he passed through a broken entryway and into a courtyard.

Sergeant Tyndall walked over to one wall, studying drawings which had been deeply incised into the sandstone before it had hardened and were still mostly visible. "Lots of horses. But they ain't drawn like the Indians do 'em."

Benton came over to look closely at the drawings, nodding in agreement. An entire herd of graven horses gamboled across the broken wall, their lines still visible despite long weathering. The horse portrayals had a fluidity which he'd never seen in the drawings which the Indian tribes produced. Then he noticed the top of the wall. Part was missing, but on the remaining portion symbols he didn't recognize had been carved in a series of long unbroken lines. "Do you recognize any of this, sergeant?"

Tyndall shook his head, looking mystified now. "No Cheyenne built this, cap'n. No, sir. And look how that sandstone's been weathered. I never seen anything built of sandstone weathered that bad. It'd take, I don't know, hundreds of years. But that's crazy. This wasn't here when we rode past last."

That tower on the hill which Garret had thought ruined hadn't been there before, either, Benton recalled. "Go get Lieutenant Garret and send him up here while you stay with the column."

"Yes, sir." Tyndall seemed glad for the chance to leave the mysterious ruins, moving as fast as the broken surfaces permitted back toward the column.

While he was waiting, Benton dug a little ways into the dirt. He found the remnants of what might have been a wooden beam, the wood long since turned to dust, but the dust blackened by the charring of fire. This place hadn't simply died. Someone had destroyed it.

Lieutenant Garret arrived, examining everything with a stupefied expression. "Captain, I had no idea the plains Indians had built anything like this."

"As far as I and the sergeant know, they didn't." Benton indicated the ruins. "You had a classical education back east, lieutenant. What do you make of this?"

Garret hesitated. "Honestly, sir?"

"You can safely assume that when I ask you something I want your honest answer, yes, lieutenant."

"Yes, sir." Garret made a helpless gesture. "It looks almost Biblical, sir. Like something from Babylon. Or maybe even a little older. The way the wall is built, what's left of the houses. I've seen paintings of what people think the Hanging Gardens looked like and they'd fit in here, sir."

"The Hanging Gardens of Babylon?" Benton decided not to make a sarcastic reply. He had asked for the lieutenant's opinion, after all. "What do you make of that?" he asked, pointing to the wall of horses and the symbols above the drawings.

Garret examined it for a long time, then shook his head. "I don't know, sir. I haven't seen art like that. Those symbols look like early writing, but I'm sure it's not cuneiform." He gave Captain Benton a worried look. "Sir, horses came to this continent with Europeans, a few centuries ago. But these depictions of horses, this whole place, feels a lot older than that."

"How old does it feel to you?" Benton asked, realizing that he agreed with the lieutenant.

Garret took a moment to think about that. "Older than anything I've ever seen, sir. Really old. A thousand years, maybe."

That sounded ridiculous, but then again saying the ruins were even a decade old, even a month old, would be equally absurd. They hadn't been here and now they were.

Picking their way out along another path, Benton paused before a deep opening which gapped in the earth, kneeling to examine it. "I think this was a salt mine. A long time ago it was a salt mine, anyway. This place must have been built around the mines, to protect them. A whole walled town grew up here." It all made sense, except that he wasn't talking about the ancient middle east but about the central Kansas prairie.

Benton wanted to have those disquieting relics out of sight, so he kept the column moving until the impossibly-old ruins were no longer visible, the cavalry reaching the low, wooded areas alongside Thompson Creek before halting for the night.

"What do you think they'll say at Fort Harker when we report that, cap'n?" Tyndall asked.

"They may call us crazy." Benton shrugged. "But they may have already heard of it. Plenty of civilians ride through this area."

"Yes, sir. I been meaning to ask you about that, cap'n." Sergeant Tyndall pursed his mouth, clearly and uncharacteristically hesitating to speak. "Where are they, sir? This area's been plenty settled in the last few years, especially since the railroad came in as far as Ellsworth. But we've seen no one else and seen none of the trails we should've crossed."

"You think everyone disappeared and that ruined city appeared in their place?"

"I don't know what happened, cap'n, but I do know that I'll be real happy when I lay eyes on Fort Harker again."

• • •

By late morning the next day even Benton was feeling extremely uneasy. They should have passed some roads and farms by now, but the only road they'd found wasn't where it should have been and seemed to have been wide and very heavily traveled in the past. Aged ruins of abandoned buildings, some still bearing the scorches of fire on their walls, were spotted near once-cultivated fields gone wild. Even stranger, another desolate tower lay tumbled to one side of the large road not far from where the cavalry column crossed it. Lieutenant Garret was sent to investigate and came back bewildered. "It's not the same architecture as the fortress ruins, sir. The tower seems sort of Roman, like the ones on Hadrian's Wall."

First the Hanging Gardens of Babylon and now Hadrian's Wall. "Kansas seems to be gaining ancient historical artifacts at a very unusual rate, lieutenant. How old is that tower, do you think?"

"It seems a lot younger than the city, sir. I'd guess it's maybe a hundred years old, or maybe two hundred. That's just a guess." Garret had been growing more and more puzzled. "Captain, are these ruins being kept secret for some reason? I've never heard a word about them."

"That's because they haven't been here, lieutenant." Feeling increasingly unsettled, Benton turned to face the column. "Mount up!" With he and his men settled into their saddles, he ordered the company into motion again, eager to see Fort Harker and the adjacent town of Ellsworth as soon as possible.

It was well after noon when they came over the last of the rises before the river lowland holding Fort Harker and Ellsworth. They had come up from the south, so both the fort and the town should have been almost due north of them. The Smoky Hill River which skirted both places was there, but otherwise the landscape was marked only by another wide road leading east. There was no sign Fort Harker or Ellsworth had ever been here, no indication the railroad line coming in from the east and then up along the Smoky Hill had ever been built here. How could an entire town and a fort with more than seventy buildings have vanished within a couple of weeks? How could the rail line and the warehouses beside it which had been there for a few years also have disappeared without a trace?

Sergeant Tyndall made a strangled sound as he looked east. Within a few miles the road entered a broad cultivated and cleared area, running through it, and up to the sealed gates of a city walled in stone which had been built between Spring Creek and Clear Creek. The city was miles east of where Ellsworth or Fort Harker should be, much bigger than either Ellsworth or the fortress to the south that they'd seen in ruins, and it was undisputedly still occupied. "Cap'n, begging your pardon, sir, but what the hell? Where's the fort and where's the town and what's that?"

"It's not Ellsworth." Benton leveled his field glasses, making out banners on the top of high walls and some sort of castle or citadel in the center of the city. "There's fighting going on. People on the walls are defending the city against a force encamped before it. See the ladders the attackers are putting up against the walls?"

Lieutenant Garret nodded, peering through his own field glasses. "Sir, I don't hear any gunshots."

Neither did he, Benton realized. Nor could he see the impossible to miss clouds of gun smoke which should have veiled the battlefield.

"What do we do, sir?" Tyndall asked.

His instructions from the colonel hadn't covered this particular set of circumstances, but they had left him the authority to use his discretion if he encountered something not mentioned in those instructions. "There's a city under attack. That's clear enough. We're to defend Ellsworth and other towns or settlers if they come under attack. That's not Ellsworth, but it's a city. We'll ride that way, evaluate the situation as we get closer, and take appropriate action."

Tyndall nodded, clearly relieved now that an officer had laid out a familiar and rational course of action.

Benton rode up close to Garret and spoke softly. "The men know something is wrong, lieutenant. They don't why any more than we do, but as long as their officers appear to be dealing with events in a calm and controlled way, the men will stay calm and controlled. Don't let the men see anything in you that might feed alarm in them. Understand?"

Lieutenant Garret nodded, his worried expression smoothing out. "Yes, sir."

The cavalry rode down from the hills to the river, splashing across and up onto the edge of the open area. The closer the column got to the walled city the more details they could make out. "They're fighting with swords," Garret announced at one point. "I think they're wearing armor, too."

Whoever had been attacking the city seemed to have noticed the cavalry company. While infantry continued to climb ladders to assail the walls, many other attackers ran back to their camp where a large herd of horses was visible, mounting up and forming into a mass facing the approaching cavalry. Benton watched the activity through his field glasses, shaking his head at the archaic armor, the brightly-colored banners and the lack of firearms. "Whoever they are, they're not dressed or armed like Indians. Neither are the people on the wall. But the city people aren't settlers like those in Ellsworth, either."

"The ones attacking the city look more hostile to me, cap'n," Tyndall commented. "It appears they're aiming to hit us, too."

"I'd prefer to parley first, but if they want a fight, they'll get it. Bugler, sound form a line." The sweet notes of the bugle resounded as the troopers in the cavalry column swung out to ride abreast, the two platoons of the company forming two lines, one behind the other, extending across a front facing the oncoming riders.

Benton halted the cavalry, standing in his stirrups and raising one empty hand high in the universal sign of parley.

The mass of horsemen facing them, now less than two miles distant, shouted what sounded like battle cries and came riding toward the cavalry without much semblance of a formation.

Captain Benton evaluated the terrain, looked at the enemy with their armor and swords, and made his decision. Experience told him that the people in the city should be settlers, and the attackers hostiles. Moreover, the attackers gave every sign of having decided to attack the cavalry as well. His company's horses were tired, there were only about one hundred men all told in the company against what seemed four or five times that number of attackers, and he wasn't about to have his soldiers trade saber blows with a mass of men wearing armor. "Lieutenant Garret, Sergeant Tyndall, form two dismounted lines of battle."

Tyndall saluted, turned to face the cavalry and bellowed his commands. "Company B, dismount! Form line of battle, first platoon front, second platoon rear!" The commands echoed along the cavalry ranks, the cavalrymen pulling their Sharps carbines from their saddle scabbards and dismounting. One of every four took control of four horses, leading them back a ways to where the wagons waited, while the remaining three soldiers fell into two long, open lines facing the enemy, the front rank kneeling and the second rank standing, each man about a yard from the men to the left and right of him. Less than a minute after Tyndall had shouted the orders, the cavalry was arrayed for battle.

Benton remained on his horse, riding slowly along the line. "Uncase the colors." Canvas tubes came off the swallow-tailed guidon of the 5th Cavalry regiment and the flag of the United States of America, the banners unfurling to flap proudly in the breeze.

The oncoming horsemen were less than half a mile away, increasing their speed to a gallop. "They're going to wear out them horses, charging that hard that far," Tyndall observed, apparently unconcerned. He'd fought at Gaines' Mill in the War of the Rebellion, and since then in dozens of other battles and skirmishes. This was just one more.

Benton raised his empty hand again. "Halt! We are United States Cavalry." He doubted those charging toward the cavalry could hear him over the sound of their own horses, and in any case the attackers seemed oddly unconcerned by the steady lines of carbines facing them.

Drawing his pistol, Benton waited as the horsemen grew closer, the earth shaking from the pounding of their horses' hooves. "Mark your man and aim your shots," he called, riding slowly across the back of the second line of dismounted cavalry. "Standby. First Platoon, fire!"

The kneeling rank fired their weapons in a rippling volley, immediately afterwards breaking open their carbines to eject the spent cartridge from the breech and reload as Benton called out his next order. "Second Platoon, fire!"

The shortest pause to allow the first rank to finish loading. "First Platoon, fire!"

"Second Platoon, fire!"

The volleys crashed out and the horses of the attackers went wild, bucking frantically, bolting and panicking. Armored men fell everywhere, some dead or wounded from hits by the heavy .50 caliber carbine bullets, other losing their seats and being hurled from the saddle by horses gone berserk. The attack had dissolved into total chaos, the survivors of the first four volleys fleeing as fast as they or their mounts could tear across the landscape.

"Company B, cease fire!"

Sergeant Tyndall stared at the remnants of the attack, shaking his head. "It's like those horses had never heard a shot fired, cap'n." His horse, like all cavalry mounts, had been trained not to flinch at the sound of gunshots. "And why can't those men keep their seats?" Then his expression cleared. "They don't have stirrups. Just like Indians. But those ain't any Indians I ever saw."

Looking past the ruin of the mounted charge, Benton could see the infantry which had been assailing the city frantically coming down off of their ladders and running through their camp, not to form a defensive line but away from the cavalry, joining their mounted comrades in panicked flight.

Sergeant Tyndall watched the rout, scratching his head. "Well, I'll be damned. I guess we won. Now what do we do, cap'n?"

Benton wished for a moment that he had someone superior in rank to ask that same question. But there seemed only one realistic course of action. "Company B, mount up." He waited until the soldiers in the rear had brought forward the horses and the cavalry once again formed two mounted lines. "Bugler, sound advance. Let's go get a better look at that city. Sergeant Tyndall, make sure the wagons close up with us."

They rode at a walk, wheeling the lines to bypass to one side of the dead and dying horsemen, but close enough for Benton to get a good look at some of them. He saw blond hair, brown hair, and black hair, skin and facial features which resembled mostly European but sometimes Asian, and weapons and armor which seemed out of the early middle ages or late Roman Empire.

This was all inexplicable, yet Benton knew he had to lead his company through whatever was going on. Already emotionally a bit numb, Benton focused tightly on the routines and procedures which needed to be followed now.

As the cavalry lines approached the city, they rode through the empty tent camp of the former besiegers, who were still visible in the distance but running for all they were worth. On the walls of the city, defenders were waving swords, spears and axes over their heads and cheering. "Company B, halt! I guess we'd better find out who these people are and where we are, sergeant. Lieutenant Garret, hold the company here while the sergeant and I go parley."

Benton rode toward the walls, Sergeant Tyndall on his horse just behind. Spotting a cluster of figures near some blue banners embroidered with many-pointed stars, Benton headed that way, assuming they would be the leaders of the defenders. Holding up his right palm again, Benton checked his horse just under the walls. Still skittish from the battle, his horse danced sideways as more cheers erupted from overhead.

Looking upward, Benton called out. "I am Captain Ulysses Benton, United States Cavalry. I wish to speak to your commanding officer, leader or chieftain."

A babble of noise broke out above in which Benton couldn't make out a single familiar word, though some of the words teased at him in the way of sounds which share the same root as a word in a known language. Then the shouts died down rapidly as one of the defenders stood up on the rampart, gazing down a good twenty feet at Benton. This person wore a chain-mail shirt, with more mail forming a hauberk around the neck, what appeared to be leather trousers, and heavy leather boots which came up to the knee, almost meeting the mail shirt where it hung down. The chain mail was torn in several places where the blows of swords or axes had struck home. On the defender's head, a bright helm topped with a white horse hair plume shone in the sun. Raising one hand to mimic Benton's gesture, the defender called down a long sentence, not one word of which Benton could understand.

But that wasn't why he stared up, momentarily shocked into silence. The leader of the defenders, face streaked with sweat and dust, sword still wet with blood, had spoken in the unmistakable voice of a woman.

All right, then. The leader of the city was a woman. Compared to the disappearances of Fort Harker and Ellsworth, that was a relatively easy thing to accept.

Behind Benton, Sergeant Tyndall made a baffled sound. The captain turned in the saddle, facing the sergeant. "Did you recognize anything she said?"

"Sir…cap'n…that's a woman!"

"It seems so, sergeant, now tell me if you recognized her language. Is it in any way related to Cheyenne or Arapaho?" He already thought he knew the answer. It hadn't sounded a bit like a plains tribe language. If anything, some of the words had sounded vaguely European.

"No, sir." Tyndall shook his head. "Not them, and not Sioux or Pawnee. I've talked to some of the civilized tribes down south, Cherokee, Choctaw and the like, and it didn't sound like none of them, neither."

"I think I'd recognize Shoshone," Benton said. "It's not Crow, either. Did it sound a little Spanish?"

"Maybe a little, sir," Sergeant Tyndall agreed. "But it's not." He scrunched up his face. "And I ain't never seen a senorita like that, cap'n."

Looking closely, Benton could now make out the feminine features under the helm. Unless he was mistaken, as many as half of the other defenders might be women as well. "Amazons. In Kansas. Maybe that's Greek they're speaking." The idea was absurd, but no more so than what he was seeing. "Lieutenant Garret!"

Garret rode up, saluting.

"You know some Greek, don't you?"

"Classical Greek, yes, sir. From Homer. Just a little."

Benton gestured upward. "Try it on her."

Gazing at the Amazon, Garret hesitatingly spoke a few words. The woman spread her hands to show she didn't understand and called down again. "Captain, I - That's strange. It almost sounds like a lot of languages, but it's none of them."

Benton tried again. "We're from Fort Harker, in the state of Kansas, United States of America." He didn't need a translator to see that no one on the wall recognized any of those names.

The woman called once more, gesturing in a way that conveyed she wanted them to wait, then hopped down inside the wall and disappeared from view. After a few minutes, the sound of heavy objects being moved came from behind the walls, then the massive gates of the city swung open and the woman came out riding toward the cavalrymen astride a horse which seemed part Arabian and part plains pony. Behind her came a small party of other mounted fighters from the city, both men and women, though those all stopped perhaps fifteen feet from the cavalrymen while the woman came on until she reined in close to them.

"No stirrups," Sergeant Tyndall murmured. "Just like the others."

Benton checked, having been distracted just watching the Amazon ride up, seeing that her saddle did lack stirrups and had high ridges in the front and back, doubtless to help the rider keep a seat during battle.

"Be careful, cap'n," Tyndall added in a low voice. "Women can be tricky."

The woman crossed her arms over her chest and bowed in her saddle, speaking again in a way which conveyed authority, then held out her hands to show what she held. "Bread and salt," Garret said in a surprised voice. "That's an ancient gesture of hospitality, captain."

"She's welcoming us?"

"Yes, sir, welcoming us as guests. You're supposed to take a little of both to show you accept the hospitality."

Benton kneed his horse forward a couple of paces, coming within easy reach of the Amazon. This close he could finally judge her age, thinking she was probably in her mid-to-late thirties, not all that different from Benton himself. Reaching carefully, Benton grasped the bread and took a bite, tasting a hearty loaf with a strange nut-like aroma which didn't match any wheat variety he had encountered. With his other hand, Benton rubbed a finger in the salt, feeling the warmth of the woman's palm under it, then raised the finger to his mouth and licked it.

She turned to hand the bread and salt to another woman who rode up hastily. This Amazon was a bit older, stouter, her armor bearing signs of long wear and careful maintenance. Something about the way she carried herself and answered the first woman's instructions made Benton glance at Sergeant Tyndall. "I think we've found the leading sergeant here."

Tyndall looked as if he couldn't decide whether to be scandalized or fascinated. But he could surely tell that Captain Benton was willing to accept the idea, so the sergeant seemed ready to follow his captain's lead here as he had so many times before.

The leader of the city pointed toward Benton again. No, not just toward him, but to his uniform blouse and trousers, and then upwards before inclining her head respectfully toward him.

"Any guesses what that's about, lieutenant?"

"No, sir."

The Amazon swept off her helm, revealing dark hair cut short above her shoulders and making it easier to see that her eyes were the blue of a stormy sea. No, definitely not an Indian, but not Greek, either. Pointing to herself, the woman said two words. "Odwan Freya."

"Her name?" Garret speculated.

"Maybe name and rank," Benton replied. "She seems to be in charge." He saluted her. "Captain Benton, ma'am."

Pointing at him, the woman repeated the words. "Kiptin Bin-tin-miim." Sergeant Tyndall coughed, doubtless covering up a laugh.

"It's just –" Benton paused, then pointed to himself. "Captain Benton."

She nodded. "Kip-tan Bin-ton." The woman extended one hand toward the city and said, "Astera."

Turning once more, the Amazon gestured out to where the fleeing enemy could still be seen, shaking her head. She covered her eyes, made a series of motions mimicking someone coming stealthily this way, then drew a flat hand across her throat and pointed toward the enemy again. "She thinks those fellows might come back tonight when they can't be seen and cut our throats, cap'n," Tyndall remarked. "We'll have to post a lot of sentries."

But the woman was pointing toward the gate, then made a gesture encompassing the entire company of cavalry, before indicating the gate once more and nodding vigorously. "Achates," she declared, once again gesturing toward the cavalry and then at everyone with her and on the walls.

"Friends?" Lieutenant Garret wondered. "She's inviting us inside, sir."

Benton thought about that. He knew what could easily happen to his troopers inside the streets of a strange city. That wasn't cavalry terrain at all, and his soldiers would be badly outnumbered by the people living here.

But they needed stables and forage for the horses, food and water and shelter for the men. The sun wasn't far from setting, and having the city walls between the cavalry and those hostiles wouldn't be a bad thing, either.

The Amazon looked steadily into his eyes, no trace of deception or hostility apparent. Drawing her sword slowly, she held it out hilt-first toward Benton.

That gesture of peaceful intent was impossible to mistake. Benton noted approvingly that the woman had obviously wiped the sword blade clean of blood before returning it to its scabbard. She knew how to take proper care of a weapon. He nodded at her, studied the width of the gate for a moment, then turned to Garret. "Lieutenant, form the company up into a column of fours, then lead the column here. We will enter the city."

"Yes, sir." Garret saluted, a gesture the Amazon watched with interest, then galloped back to the cavalry. A moment later the bugler sounded the signal, the clear tones echoing from the walls of the city, and the cavalry moved quickly from their two lines into a column, four men abreast, first platoon to the front and second platoon to the rear, the wagons taking their places in the center of the column again.

The woman had resheathed her sword and now watched the

cavalry form up, an approving smile appearing on her lips. Holding up her arms, she made a fist with one hand and pounded it repeatedly into her other palm. "Extos!" she cried.

Other men and women from the city made the same gestures, which struck Benton as applause, some calling "extos" as well. The open admiration for how well his cavalry drilled helped dispel Benton's doubts.

As the head of the company reached him, Benton kneed his mount ahead to take up position in the lead. It wasn't until he turned to ride along with the column that Benton realized the Amazon had followed and now rode beside him as the cavalry approached the gateway. As they reached the gates, the guards there raised their weapons in salute to the woman and stood aside for the cavalry. The road inside jogged sharply to the right between towering walls, then led through a second gate and into the city proper. The inhabitants of the city, some still armored and carrying weapons and others either too young or too old to defend the walls, lined the broad street leading into the city, many making the fist pounding into their hand gesture.

Lieutenant Garret was looking around as if astounded. "Captain, it's like an ancient city. The walls, the weapons, the defensive arrangements, the buildings, the people, everything."

Benton heard the cheering rise in volume behind him and looked to see that the national colors had just entered to city. The inhabitants were pointing to the banner excitedly. "They recognize the flag. Thank God, they recognize the flag." He called out to the crowd, "United States of America!" several times.

But the city's people stared back blankly, before pointing at the U.S. flag and chanting "asteri" and then pointing upwards.

Lieutenant Garret understood first. "Asteri. Astra. Stars. Like the name of the city, Astera. They must consider stars important, so they're excited to see the stars on our flag."

"That big flag of theirs had a lot of stars on it, too," Sergeant Tyndall agreed.

"And our uniforms, captain," Garret continued. "She made special note of your uniform. Light blue trousers and dark blue blouse."

"The color of the sky." Hope died in Benton as quickly as it had blossomed.

"We're not in Kansas, that's for certain."

But Sergeant Tyndall was shaking his head. "I don't know what this is, cap'n, and I don't know who these folks are, but that land out there is the land around Fort Harker and Ellsworth. I'd swear to it. I just don't know where those places went and where this one came from."

Kansas but not Kansas. "Lieutenant Garret, Sergeant Tyndall, we have to make every effort to learn the language of these people, or teach them ours, well enough to find out where we really are and how to get home."

The barracks to which the cavalry was led were clean and built of stone, as were the stables for their horses. Sergeant Tyndall, accompanied by the stout Amazon, actually seemed impressed. "Real nice quarters, sir, and they seem to know how to take care of horses. I got across to Belisa what our horses needed and she made sure it all showed up fast."

"Belisa?" Benton asked.

"Uh…" Tyndall indicated the stout Amazon. "She…uh…seems pretty capable, cap'n."

After he explained with gestures to Odwan Freya that he wanted to stay with his men, Benton found himself and Lieutenant Garret offered private rooms, plainly but practically furnished. Before the men and Benton were even settled in their quarters some of the city folk were coming with large kettles filled with hot food. The dishes served, which seemed to be mostly a kind of beef mixed with grains and dried fruits, were unfamiliar but none of the famished cavalrymen turned up their noses at the food.

Odwan Freya came by to ensure the cavalry had been well taken of just as the bugler reported to Captain Benton. "Sir, do I sound taps?"

Benton looked at Freya, and nodded. "Yes. Let these people hear taps."

The bugler saluted, then marched out into the hallway and raised his instrument to his lips as Odwan Freya watched. When the last long, slow notes of General Dan Butterfield's tune had sounded, her face reflected astonishment and admiration. Turning to Benton before she left, Freya inclined her head and spoke in a quiet tone appropriate to the music she had heard. "Extos."

The next morning, Benton resolved to send Lieutenant Garret out with a squad to collect the brass from the battle. He had yet to see any sign of gunpowder weapons here, and the inhabitants of the city regarded the cavalry's carbines and pistols with an undisguised awe which seemed to reflect total unfamiliarity and suspicious fear in combination. The cavalry might end up having to make their own reloads, and while lead was easy enough to form into bullets, the brass cartridge casings wouldn't be simple to replace.

But Benton had barely eaten breakfast when Odwan Freya, along with the Amazon he increasingly thought of as 'Sergeant" Belisa, and two men came by, Freya indicating they wished him to accompany them. Collecting Lieutenant Garret and Sergeant Tyndall, Benton followed the Asterans a short distance to a large room letting out onto what seemed to be a parade ground. A line of guards stood sentry outside, not watching the cavalry but facing outward to hold back the crowds of city people who were gathered outside the barracks.

Freya pointed to the two men. "Decires Agani, Decires Costoni." Decires was obviously a title of some kind, and both men appeared to be soldiers. Both also deferred to Freya, so the Odwan must outrank them.

Agani and Belisa unrolled a large sheet of vellum onto a table filling the center of the room, pinning down the corners with polished stone blocks and looking at Benton expectantly. "Lieutenant Garret. What do you make of this?"

Garret peered at the drawing. "It's a map, captain."

"Very good. A map of what?"

The lieutenant flushed slightly at the dry rebuke, then studied the beautifully hand-drawn map intently. "They're tapping that symbol. It must be this city. Yes, that matches the river and the hills, doesn't it?"

Sergeant Tyndall, peering over Garret's shoulder, nodded. "Right, lieutenant."

Encouraged by the sergeant's agreement, Garret spoke with more confidence. "Then this over here must be the Missouri River. Which would make this the Mississippi River. And this area would be down near New Orleans. They show a town of some sort there. But many of the cities east of here seem to be missing, and these political boundaries don't match anything I know of."

"I follow you so far," Benton agreed, his own hand tracing the way west. "And this is the west coast. California. Look at all of those cities. It's as if the continent was settled first in the west and then settlers moved east."

Garret was following the west coast line north, then halted. "Sir? This goes into the new Alaska territory, but look. It just keeps going west up here. They show a broad strip of land going west until it reaches this other land mass. That's got to be Asia, captain."

"A land bridge? That big?"

The lieutenant had gone pale, his breaths coming rapidly. "Sir, sir, look. It is a land bridge. They're saying that North and South America are connected to Asia and Europe by this big isthmus."

"They're not," Benton said, wondering why Garret was getting upset.

"The map seems accurate as to terrain, sir. As far as we know. Except there."

"I'll grant you that."

"Look at these people, sir! They're not Indians. They're like Central Europeans or something, maybe with more Asian in their blood. In our history, there wasn't any easy way from Asia and Europe to North and South America, so every human migration headed west and ended in Europe. But here they could go east, too, and some of them did. Nothing we know is here. Instead there's the ruins we found, the language these people speak, the weapons and armor they carry, this city…"

A terrible suspicion filled Benton. "Are you saying what I think you're saying, lieutenant?"

"This isn't our *world*, captain." Garret seemed ready to pass out. "We haven't just lost Fort Harker. We lost our entire world. History changed somehow while we were on that patrol, but it didn't include us. There's never been a United States of America. There's probably never been an England, or a France. North America was never isolated from the rest of the world. People did colonize the west coast first, maybe thousands of years before Columbus found the Americas in our world."

"Great God Almighty," Benton murmured. He didn't want to believe such an outlandish thing, but Ellsworth and the fort were gone, ancient ruins rested where nothing had been before, and this city didn't belong to any history of which he had ever heard. Nor did Freya belong in the North America he knew, a woman wearing armor, leading her people and wielding a sword in battle, as if Joan of Arc had lived in Kansas of all places. How could such a thing have happened though? His mind seized on the memory of the moment after which nothing but the land had been familiar, and the land itself had undergone tiny changes. "That lightning during the storm. For an instant it felt as if it were tearing the world apart. Maybe it did. If you're right, lieutenant, what happened to the Indians?"

"Probably the sort of thing that happened to the first inhabitants of places like England in our history, sir. They were either wiped out by waves of invaders or assimilated, with maybe a few survivors pushed into areas no one else wanted."

The idea was impossible. But so was this city. So were these people. He wasn't an ignorant man. How could such a place exist anywhere on Earth and he not have heard of it? If it did, why did the land so closely resemble the land he knew, and how had the company of cavalry been transported there instantly without its knowledge?

Lieutenant Garret's theory was impossible, but explained what they had found here. Every other explanation required ignoring the evidence of their senses.

Freya had been watching Benton and Garret talk, and now gestured to the map, and then to Benton, clearly asking him to show where he was from.

That should have been an easy enough question to answer, but as Benton gazed at the map he realized every possible answer had problems. Strictly speaking, if Lieutenant Garret was right, then he and his cavalry company weren't "from" anywhere which existed in this world.

This city was near where Fort Harker had stood. That answer was probably as good as any other. So Benton pointed to the city.

Freya shook her head patiently, pointing to herself and then the city symbol, then to Benton, Garret, and Tyndall before waving her hand over the map again with a questioning look.

Benton pointed to the city once more, firmly, keeping his eyes on her.

She looked annoyed, then something seemed to dawn on her and Freya spoke rapidly to the other Asterans. The two men, Agani and Costoni, spoke back just as fast, their faces lighting with enthusiasm.

Freya pointed to herself and tapped her city's symbol again, nodding anxiously to Benton. He tapped himself and then the same symbol as well, nodding resolutely in return. With a dazzling smile,

Freya drew her sword and raised it overhead, shouting so loudly it echoed through the room. The other Asterans did the same, and outside Benton could hear the cries being repeated, followed by prolonged cheering from the crowds. Belisa turned to Sergeant Tyndall, hugged him, then planted a kiss on his mouth while Tyndall looked startled. The two Asteran men had grabbed Lieutenant Garret and were almost shaking him as they smiled and spoke quickly and incomprehensibly. Sheathing her sword, Freya stepped close to Benton, her eyes shining, reaching one hand to seize his upper arm in a comradely grip and squeeze so hard it hurt. "Achates! Cronun t'achates!"

"Cap'n?" Sergeant Tyndall asked. "What did you just tell 'em?"

"I'm not sure, sergeant."

"Whatever it was, it sure made 'em happy."

It took several days before Lieutenant Garret had learned enough of the Asterans' language, and they had learned enough English, to be able to provide the answer. "We've been asked to a meeting, sir, to formalize our alliance with the city state of Astera."

Benton gave Garret a questioning look. "Our alliance? Did you promise them something?"

"No, sir. You did, sir. As best I can tell, these people think we're a wandering tribe of sorts, warriors who've been kicked out of our own lands for reasons they're too polite to ask about. When Odwan Freya asked where you were from and you kept pointing to this city on the map, they decided that meant we had decided to settle here, to join forces with them."

No wonder the Asterans had been so happy. From what little they'd been able to learn so far, the cavalry company was like nothing in this world. Benton looked out across the parade ground. "That wasn't what I meant, lieutenant, but maybe that's not a bad idea."

Garret nodded unhappily. "We don't seem to have anywhere else to go."

"No. Here we have shelter, food, walls to protect us, and civilized people who need us." He blew out a long breath. "Damn. Part of me says we should ride until we reach the east coast if necessary, confirm with our own eyes that Fort Riley and Fort Leavenworth and St. Louis and Chicago and Pittsburgh and Washington, D.C. aren't there any more and never were there. But another part of me already knows the answer. This is the area around Ellsworth. We couldn't mistake the terrain. But there's never bee n an Ellsworth here, never been a Fort Harker. Instead there's sandstone quarries and salt mines dating back a thousand years."

The lieutenant shook his head this time, his eyes haunted by worry. "I've been learning everything I can, captain, and I still haven't found anything the least bit familiar in the history of this place."

"Me, neither." There'd been assorted city-states over the last thousand years, empires rising and falling apart, the latest such an empire which had its capital where San Francisco should be and had covered most of the land between the west coast up to about where the Oregon Territory lay, south into Mexico, and as far east as the Mississippi. But that empire, which had built the watch towers, had slowly disintegrated over the course of the last century, leaving city states squabbling over the remnants. "I can't find out much about Europe, and they barely seem to know anything about Africa."

"Yes, sir. They don't know much about either place. I'd wager there are settlements from Europe on the east coast, but these people don't have much knowledge of what's east of the Appalachians." Garret looked around as if evaluating the city again. "The technology here is a millennium behind ours, captain. No gunpowder, no steam power, no printing presses. They seem just as intelligent as we are, I swear they're learning our language faster than we're learning theirs, so maybe people just got started later here somehow."

"Or they didn't advance as fast for other reasons." He recalled that the stirrup had come into the Roman Empire along with some of those barbarian invaders from the east. How many innovations, how much progress, had been because of those migrations all dead-ending in Europe? If some of them had gone east instead, would progress have been slower everywhere? "Or maybe a combination of those things. There doesn't appear to be any way home, though."

"No, sir." Garret squinted at the city around them. "We're actually already there, it's just not the same there."

"Corporal Fuller is impressed by the local blacksmiths."

"What about ammunition, captain?"

"It turns out Private Merrick worked in a powder mill as a boy. He even remembers the right proportions for the ingredients. These people have a lot of livestock so getting saltpeter won't be a problem, and charcoal is easy enough to come by. We just have to explain what sulfur is and see if the locals can provide that. Our saddlemaker is busy showing the Asterans how to make stirrups. We'll have to see how long we can keep the advantages of stirrups and gunpowder confined to Astera."

Lieutenant Garret looked impressed and concerned. "You seem to have thought out what we need to do, to stay here a long time."

"It's my job to think things out, lieutenant." Benton sighed. "And we both have to assume that we're going to be here quite a while. A few of the men were married. I still haven't worked out how to tell them we're on permanent campaign."

"Maybe we'll be like Odysseus, sir, and have some strange adventures but make it home eventually."

"Maybe."

The negotiations were hard, rendered difficult both by the still limited language both sides shared and by the Asterans' apparent insistence on driving what they thought a fair bargain. At one point, as Garret and Costoni spent an extended conversation trying to figure out what each other meant, Benton saw Odwan Freya giving him a hard look and comprehended that he had been gazing at her for a while without realizing it.

Now Freya said some things, and Costoni said some things, and Garret went back and forth with them for a while before turning a worried glance on Benton. "Captain, I'm pretty certain that they're insisting that Odwan Freya is not part of the deal."

"What? What does that mean?"

"Ancient treaties were often sealed by marriages or, uh, other arrangements, sir."

Benton's reaction must have showed, because the Asterans seemed to lose some of their tense watchfulness. "Tell her - No, I have to say this directly to her. Odwan Freya, please accept my apologies for any implied inappropriate interest on my part. I would never…make your person a part of any agreement. You are the leader of these people and a free woman, and I would not so insult you as to barter for you. My country recently fought a terrible war, one which only ended five years ago, and in which many thousands of men died in order to establish the principle that no human being should ever belong to another, ever be bought or sold or treated as property. I am sworn to uphold those principles in my professional duties, and I personally believe deeply in them."

He had no idea how much of that Odwan Freya and the other Asterans had understood, but enough seemed to have gotten across. Freya nodded to him, then surprised Benton by rendering him a passable imitation of a regulation salute. Benton returned the gesture, knowing neither of them had made it in a subservient way, but as mutual gestures of respect among equals.

The people here did not campaign in the cold season, so the company settled in to wait out the frigid fury of the plains winter in a degree of comfort unheard of for them. The men remained baffled as to where they were, but content to be living in comparative luxury among a citizenry who almost worshiped them. Benton continued to apply himself to learning the Asterans' language, but found that just as Garret had said the Asterans seemed more adept at learning English. Aside from getting home, the security situation concerned Benton the most, so he questioned Freya about it as her grasp of his language improved.

"The army that was attacking Astera, the Wikosans." Wikosa occupied roughly the same location as Kansas City had in Benton's world. "Do you know why they attacked us without talking first?"

"Bad people, Wikosans," Freya responded.

"But why did they assume we were enemies? Why did they try to ride us down?"

Freya seemed to think about the question this time before answering. "You get off horse. All walk, make long, thin line. Not many of you. They think, ride over you. Easy. Then bwam, bwam! Smoke and fire, like demons."

Of course. Like the British infantry square, troops armed with pikes or spears would have had to be tightly packed, shoulder to shoulder, in order to defend against a mounted charge. Modern firearms changed that, but the hostile horsemen hadn't known of such weapons. To them the thin line of dismounted cavalry must have looked extremely vulnerable.

The more they learned about Astera the more Benton realized that whichever fate had led them here had at least sent them to a people deserving of rescue. Astera had grown large and fairly well-off during the period when the last empire kept the peace on the plains. Trade had flowed along the road running east and west, and there had been major routes going north and south accessible through Wikosa. The surrounding area had boasted numerous farms and fields with a variety of livestock. But since the collapse of the empire Astera had suffered from the loss of trade and the unstable security outside its walls. Nonetheless, the city had remained a bastion of learning, order and civilization in a region where such things had become all too rare.

The Wikosans, on the other hand, had tried to maintain their city's wealth by plundering surrounding regions, something which had worked in the short term but now required them to range farther and farther afield since the communities near them had been looted dry.

"Cap'n, sir?" Sergeant Tyndall asked awkwardly a few weeks after their arrival. "We got a situation that needs handling. Private Murphy keeps asking me when we're going to hold church services."

He should have realized the troopers of Irish descent would worry about that more than the others. "Have you found any Catholic priests, sergeant?"

"No, sir. What do I tell Murphy and the others?"

"Let me talk to the Odwan, first." He wasn't surprised to learn from Freya that the Catholic church didn't exist as such in this world, or at least in this part of this world, but on the other hand the Asterans had no objection to others practicing their own beliefs as long as such beliefs didn't involve human sacrifice. Benton informed his troopers that they could hold services as they wished and that he would officiate at any of them if asked.

The next crisis was one Benton had assumed was inevitable. Sergeant Tyndall escorted Private Bannock into Benton's quarters, the Asteran "Sergeant" Belisa hovering in the background with an unreadable expression. With a worried glance at Tyndall, Bannock saluted. "Captain, request permission to marry, sir."

"What happened, sergeant?" Benton asked Tyndall.

"Thanks to Bannock, one of the city girls is in a family way, captain. Belisa tells me the girl's family is okay with that, as long as Bannock does his duty by her."

The Asteran nodded soberly. "He binds to her, and her only. Marriage? Yes. Or he pays child-price."

"What's child-price?"

"Enough to take care of child until grown."

Private Bannock owned little but the uniform on his back, and that was technically the property of the U.S. Government. Benton gave Bannock a sharp look. "You plan on marrying her? Do you understand that this will be a legal marriage that you can't just ride away from?"

"Yes, sir."

"Do you have any idea what I'll do to you if I find out you have in any way mistreated that girl or acted in any way which might disappoint the people of this city in our company or damage the reputation of the United States Cavalry?"

"Yes, sir. No, sir. I'll treat her right, sir."

"Permission granted."

The cavalry company hunkered down within the city as winter hit hard, the winds howling from the north and snow drifts piling up against the walls of the city so deep in places that groups of citizens were sent out to clear them before anyone could use the drifts as ramps to enter the city.

His language skills improving daily, Benton found he could speak more and more naturally with Freya in a strange mix of English and the Asteran tongue. The Odwan had proven skilled at working out any conflicts among the cavalry and the city, mediating in a way which had impressed Benton. Lieutenant Garret, when not helping to supervise the company and its efforts to become self-sufficient, spent a lot of time in the city's library, puzzling his way through documents some of which were written in languages the Asterans themselves had little command of.

Unfortunately, the more they learned the more obvious it was that one company of cavalry couldn't miraculously solve all of the problems here. The Asterans had been able to use diplomacy to play different potential foes off of each other. This had limited attacks on the city, but as the experience with the Wikosans had shown even the most Byzantine diplomacy had its limits when it couldn't be backed up by sufficient power. Astera's position remained perilous, cut off from trade and with many crops and much livestock lost to the same Wikosans who had attacked the city. It would take time to get a gunpowder mill set up and a steady source of sulfur identified, and until then the cavalry was limited to the ammunition they had brought with them. The idea of equipping the Asterans with rifles manufactured here had been raised early on, but the city simply didn't have enough of the right metals and tools to even produce more than a few such weapons on a hand-crafted basis over the winter.

On a crisp day in what Benton thought was January, a once-more awkward Sergeant Tyndall stopped by. "Begging your pardon, cap'n. But there's something I've been wondering. You see, sir, there's a lot about this place that's different, and sometimes it takes a while to figure if different is good different or bad different or just something you can make either way."

Benton nodded solemnly. "I suppose that's right, sergeant."

"Well, cap'n, an old Indian once told me that when the great spirit gives you a horse, you don't go around looking for another dog instead. What I mean is, even if something isn't the way you always thought things should be, maybe it's still okay."

"Is that about Belisa, sergeant?"

Tyndall's face flushed red. "Yes, sir, cap'n."

"Do you want to know if it's okay to get to know her better?"

"I think I already know her real well, cap'n. Not to imply anything improper. No, sir." The sergeant let exasperation show. "But, cap'n, come campaign season, if the Asteran army goes out, Belisa goes with it. She's made it real clear that won't change. At first I was thinking, all right, Tyndall, you'll rescue the lady if she needs it. But I've watched Belisa training and practice fighting an' all, and now I'm thinking it's just as likely she might be the one rescuing me. And I don't know what to think about all that, sir. Her fighting in a battle and being real good at it. She's a fine top sergeant as well as a fine woman, cap'n. But that ain't what I was brought up thinking a woman should be."

It was the sort of question he had thought would have arisen more than it already had. "Sergeant, I've already given considerable consideration to just that question. I believe it comes down to this. You appreciate the woman who Belisa is. If she were a different woman, would you think the same of her?"

Tyndall scratched his head. "I don't know for sure, cap'n. Maybe not. She wouldn't be Belisa. Now, she wasn't raised a Christian, either, but that don't bother me. The Good Lord understands that kind of thing, and Belisa seems a better Christian than many a church-goer I've seen, if you take my meaning, sir."

"Then, Sergeant," Benton advised, "I'd tell you to take Belisa as she is. She's not what we were raised to expect, but she is, as you say, a fine woman. Maybe changing what we expect isn't a bad idea."

Grinning, Tyndall nodded. "Yes, sir. Thank you, sir. That's the truth, isn't it? Though she's not the only fine woman here. Not by a long shot. That Odwan Freya, she'd make a fine officer's lady. Hell, I mean she's a fine officer in her own right. Oh, damnation, what I mean is –"

"I understand, sergeant." After Tyndall had left, Benton sat thinking, surprised at his own reactions to the sergeant's words about Freya. She was a fine lady, indeed, and the more he learned of her the more he thought of her. But his inadvertent implication at the negotiations that he might use her need for the cavalry's support to force her favors had been bothering Benton ever since then. Surely Freya had not forgotten, either. As an officer and as a gentleman, he could not allow her to believe that he ever intended demanding her self as a price for the protection the cavalry company provided the city.

Only a few days later, Freya asked him to speak privately with her. The weather was mild that day, so she led the way to the city walls, where they could stand on a rampart isolated from anyone else and speak knowing that no one was close enough to overhear.

Freya leaned on the wall, looking east. She wasn't dressed for battle, but wearing one of the outfits in which she usually conducted business, a white blouse embroidered with depictions of horses which seemed to bear some ancestral debt to the drawings in the ruins south of here, dark trousers with more embroidery in many colors, a long over-skirt split almost all the way up the center and back so it fell gracefully at rest but didn't hinder movement or riding, and over all a high-collar, knee-length coat with more needle-work, this time of warriors and battles moving among signs and emblems of various kinds. It wasn't like any outfit which Benton had ever seen a woman wear, yet he found it very pleasing to the eye. "We must speak of war," Freya said. "The Wikosans plan to attack Astera again, as soon as the threat of freezing storms lessens, but before we expect them."

"Your scouts told you this?"

"Yes. Scouts. Spies. I think both words are right. They say the army will be at least ten decires strong."

"Decires? I thought that was a military rank."

"Decires are also those who lead decires." Freya held up her hands, all fingers spread, then closed all but two.

"Twelve?"

"A decire is a twelve of twelves."

Benton did the math. "One hundred and forty-four. Ten of those. So about one thousand five hundred." Very nasty odds if only his cavalry company was counted, but Astera had its own army. "How many soldiers do you have?"

"Able to defend the walls? About eight decires. The ones who could face the enemy in open battle only number about six decires, though."

A question had kept occurring to him, and now he voiced it. "What happened? There's a lot more young and elderly people in this city than there are men and women of military age, and you had plenty of room for my men in your barracks and for our horses in your stables."

Freya's face grew somber and she let out a long sigh, her forehead resting for a moment on the cold stone of the parapet before she raised it again. "The last Odwan gathered the largest force which Astera could muster, and marched it to meet Wikosa in battle. He didn't know the Wikosans had forged a temporary alliance with Telasa, which controls the lands south of us to the great gulf. As our army fought the Wikosans, the Telasans fell upon us from the rear." She shook her head. "Some of us managed to hold our formations together and fight our way clear. If night hadn't fallen we wouldn't have gotten away, but under cover of darkness we escaped. We left many comrades behind, those who had died holding their places. Now you know why we greeted your alliance with such joy."

It must have been a battle rivaling some of those during the southern rebellion against the United States. "The alliance has benefited us as well. How many mounted troops do you have?"

"Half a decire. Brave, but not the equal of yours, even if you did not carry the carbines."

All right, then. About one hundred U.S. Cavalry, counting all ranks, against fifteen hundred enemy soldiers. "We can fight on horse or on foot, outside the walls or inside, depending on what seems best."

"It is wise not make firm plans until we know more." But despite her words Freya appeared unhappy, and she finally faced him full on. "I have deceived you in part. Not by saying what is false, but by not saying all that is true."

Benton frowned at her, shocked by how badly that statement had rattled him.

"There can be no half-truths between us if we are to fight as one," Freya continued. "Now, under the sky, I give you a full answer to what you asked before. You wondered why the Wikosans attacked your troop without speaking first, without learning who you were. That was my doing."

That had been the last thing which Benton had expected to hear. "You told the Wikosans to attack us? And they did?"

"No, no! Not that way. They would have heeded nothing from me. But on the walls we saw you coming. We could tell even from a distance that you weren't from any place we knew of. We had nothing to lose. I ordered everyone on the walls to begin cheering and pointing toward you, as if you were expected allies who had come to relieve the siege of the city."

He stared now, momentarily wordless at Freya's audacity. "You fooled the Wikosans into thinking you were happy to see us and that we were coming to help you?"

"We *were* happy to see you," Freya replied with a half smile, "and you *were* coming to relieve the city. You just didn't know it yet." The smile grew and became mischievous before fading into regret. "I should have told you. But I feared your response, and Astera needs your cavalry so badly."

He really ought to be angry that she had provoked the Wikosans to attack his company, but Benton found himself laughing. "That was a stratagem worthy of U.S. Grant himself! Sergeant Tyndall was right when we first met you and he told me to watch out for tricks from you." Only after the last sentence had left his mouth did Benton realize he shouldn't have said that to her.

But Freya didn't seem offended, instead smiling. "You must thank your sergeant for me for giving me such praise."

Praise? Well, why wouldn't she see it that way? Male commanders who outwitted their opponents by using clever tricks, or stratagems, were happy to be praised for such skills. Why wouldn't a woman commander feel the same way? "I'll be sure to tell him you were pleased."

"Who is this U.S. Grant? Your leader?"

"Yes. He was a general, a war leader, and he was recently elected our president. That is, the people of my country voted for him to lead us."

"Oh. An Odwan. Like me."

"You?" Benton found himself staring at Freya again. "I thought you were some sort of princess." Caught up with learning about the past here, learning the language and keeping an eye on the company, he'd neglected to learn much about how the city was run. It simply hadn't been necessary when he could deal directly with Odwan Freya.

"Prin-cess?" she now asked.

"Yes. Hereditary royalty. Your family rules because they're always in charge."

Freya's smile vanished. "Don't you believe I could earn this position on my own? Be elected because I'm the best at it?"

He could feel the heat of an embarrassed flush on his face as he realized that was exactly what his thoughts had been, even though Freya had repeatedly proven her intelligence and skills as a leader. "My sincere apologies. I spoke without thinking."

She seemed uncertain whether to accept the apology. "Our people belong to groups. By where they live, by what they do for work. The groups elect leaders, who form the council. The council votes for the Odwan."

A form of democracy then, instead of the monarchal set-up he had assumed. "I am sorry."

Freya gave Benton a direct look. "Why did you think otherwise? Your men, they seemed surprised by our women. I did not wish to pry, but now I ask why?"

"Because back home our women don't fight alongside men and don't hold positions of authority."

Her gaze sharpened. "Unless they are a prin-cess?"

"Yes."

"This is a very backward place you come from. I had thought it very civilized, but now I see otherwise."

He bit back an angry rebuttal. *Backward? When we have carbines and pistols and you have bows and arrows? But she's not talking about weapons, or technology. She's talking about…civilization.*

When he was twelve years old, Benton's mother had drawn

up and proposed a few changes in the laws of his hometown. His mother, well read and with a keen mind, had crafted ideas which had impressed twelve-year old Ulysses Benton, and which he still thought would have been of great benefit to the town. However, the proposals had been rejected without discussion or debate, but with a goodly portion of scorn because they had been made by a woman. His mother had never again ventured to do such a thing, though he had seen the well-hidden resentment in her whenever politics was discussed in her hearing, and young Benton had often wondered that the most foolish and least educated man in town could vote in elections and his mother could not.

He thought of the West he had known with a different way of seeing it, thinking of the women there who from necessity or desire worked at tasks regarded as unfeminine by his civilization. That civilization had not yet established a firm grip on those who lived between the Missouri River and the Sierra Nevada Mountains, and Benton now realized for the first time that when that happened, and women in the West were confined to corsets and kitchens, something of great value would have been lost. *Maybe changing what we expect isn't a bad idea*, he had told Sergeant Tyndall. "You have a point there. You have a very good point there."

His response finally seemed to mollify Freya. "But you do not truly think like that. I see this. For a moment I feared you were like the Wikosans."

"They're that different from your people?" Benton asked.

Freya pointed west. "We are from those who came out of Palenkaza long ago. Along the waters of the greatest ocean."

"The west coast."

"Yes. The lands there. We, the peoples to our south and west and some ways north, all came out of Palenkaza, where the men and women work as one. This is as our ancestors were and as the Light wishes. But the Wikosans are of those who came out of Bareos, from the north out of the cold lands. They, and the people north and east of them to the mountains, do not live as we do."

Waves of migration, as Lieutenant Garret had speculated. "They don't have women soldiers?"

"Of course they do! What city could stand if half of its people didn't bear arms along with the other half? But the Wikosans use their women only to guard the city. On the attack, they use men, and they allow no women to lead their armies."

It felt odd to know that he would have agreed without question with the Wikosans not long ago, and even odder to realize how much his opinions of women had changed from being around those of Astera.

Freya inclined her head toward him. "Do I have your forgiveness for my deception?"

"Yes, Odwan Freya. I respect you all the more that you admitted to it, and for the cleverness of your stratagem. But you're right that we must keep each other apprised of such stratagems in the future."

She smiled, and Benton realized she had really cared how he would react. But then, the safety of her city and her people rested on how he had accepted the news, didn't it?

Six weeks later, a courier raced down the road from the east, bringing news that triggered a full council of war. Besides Freya and Benton, it included Lieutenant Garret, the Decires Agani and Costoni, Sergeant Tyndall and Belisa.

Decire Agani laid out the news brought by the rider. "They come early, before their full force is ready, to strike us with surprise when we believe ourselves still safe. The Wikosans number only about six decires. This is a great opportunity. We can strike them and wipe them out."

Freya ran her hands across the map before them, tapping an area which Benton estimated was about twenty five miles to the east-northeast of Astera, near where Salina had been. "We could do it here, near the crossroads." She frowned. "Why do I feel doubts?"

Benton glanced at Lieutenant Garret, who gestured at the map. "It seems like a perfect opportunity, sir."

Sergeant Tyndall cleared his throat, and Benton turned his gaze that way. "What do you think, sergeant?"

Tyndall squinted at the map, his mouth twisting. "Captain, an old Indian once told me that when you see one wolf, you ought to be wondering where the rest of the pack is."

Lieutenant Garret frowned in puzzlement, but Freya gave the sergeant a careful look. "You think this is a trap? Why?"

"Ma'am, I'm no general, but I'm looking at these guys and there ain't all that many of them. They out-number us, sure, but even if we didn't have our carbines we'd still be in a fort. I'm thinking, what if they're bait? The Indians do that, send out a few braves to lure us into chasing them and then before you know it there's a lot more Indians on all sides."

Belisa was nodding. "The Telasans. Like last time."

"The Telasans cannot come north this early in the year." Decira Agani pointed at the map. "If we fail always to act, we will never win. This is a great opportunity."

"True," Freya agreed. "But the chance seems too good. Are the Wikosans so foolish? They know we have the carbines of the cavalry now."

"Our messenger says the Wikosan fighters have been told it was a trick, a noise to frighten them but one otherwise harmless."

"They'll learn otherwise," Tyndall remarked with a grin.

"But," Benton added, "their own leaders may have convinced themselves it's true. Those killed by our shots didn't make it home."

Freya nodded. "They were buried on the field in one grave. So, the Wikosans believe us to be desperate and still weak. They would think this bait would be irresistible. We could not risk not taking it.

It is in my mind to find the hook, that which would strike us when we go for the bait, and to deal the surprise to them."

Benton was studying the terrain. "Will they expect you to attack them in that place you showed us?"

"There or closer to Astera. No farther off, because we would not risk such a long march from our city, leaving it lightly defended in our absence."

"I can see a crossroads, but is there a town there? What do these symbols mean?" Salina had boasted a population of about one thousand, but it was surely gone along with every other human artifact he had known of in Kansas.

Costoni shook his head. "The ruins of a city. Over there, to the northeast of the crossroads. It's been empty for a very long time. Right there, not far away from the ruins, there was a town in the time of the empire, but it was new and too small to defend itself when the empire fell, and was abandoned as well a few decades ago."

Benton nodded, trying not to let what he had known of human habitation in that area get in the way of what was now there. "There's not a lot of cover on the plains, but a force moving along a watercourse would be low and screened by the trees growing alongside the water." He moved one finger the length of a stream. "Is this Spring Creek, sergeant?"

"Yes, sir."

"This would offer a great approach for that hook you spoke of, Odwan Freya. They could move along here, concealed from being spotted by anyone on the road roughly paralleling them to south."

The Asterans followed his gesture, nodding. "Six decires on the road," Decire Costoni remarked. "That leaves at least four for the hook. I distrust our reports on this. If the Wikosans gathered even minor help from cities such as Lacanan," he pointed to near where St. Louis should be, "or Midasa," pointing to a place about midway between Omaha and Sioux City, "they could easily have at least six decires in the hook, or perhaps another hook to the south as well." Costoni pointed to a another watercourse running south of the area. "What do you call this?"

"Dry Creek," Tyndall replied. "Cap'n, if someone followed Dry Creek where it bends west, it'd take 'em toward that same area with Spring Creek to the north."

"Cannae?" Lieutenant Garret wondered. "That's what Hannibal did at Cannae, tricking the Romans into attacking and then surrounding them on both flanks."

"None of us would escape this time," Freya murmured, her expression as she looked at the map becoming concentrated like that of a cougar eyeing her prey. "But we are not so desperate as they think. If we turn their own plan upon them, Wikosa will suffer such a blow that for years they will be busy defending themselves from those they have preyed upon." Her hand moved as she talked, sketching out movements of forces, while the others watched and listened, Benton with growing approval, Garret obviously surprised but listening closely, the two Decires nodding, and Tyndall's own jaw slowly dropping.

As they left the room, Sergeant Tyndall shook his head. "What do you think, cap'n?"

"I think it's bold and has a decent chance of success." Benton smiled. "I once compared Odwan Freya to U.S. Grant. I guess I was more right than I knew."

"U.S. Grant? Hell, cap'n, if she pulls this off she'll be Grant, Sherman and Sheridan all rolled into one."

The Asterans had developed fairly decent weather forecasting ability, being as reliant on the skill as any people who depended on grazing, farming and trade for their survival. When the forecasters declared a mild period was coming up, Freya ordered the Asteran forces to prepare to march at any time. Captain Benton took his company out on the field before the city and drilled them out of their winter ease, getting the cavalry ready for offensive operations.

Additional mounted scouts were sent out in all directions. The city could ill afford to spare them from its battle forces, but it would need all the warning time it could get if any other enemy army came marching toward the city from an unexpected route.

When word came down the road that the Wikosans were coming, and with the predicted six decires, the Asterans and the cavalry set out. Benton looked up at the walls as they rode away, seeing many young women waving to his soldiers, and they waving back.

"Just like old times," Sergeant Tyndall commented. "Remember riding off in 1861?"

"Yes, sergeant, I do. We were going to have the rebellion crushed before the year was out. That's what they said, anyway."

"Things don't always work out like we plan." Tyndall looked over to where the Asteran column was marching, accompanied by the small Asteran mounted force. The saddles of the Asteran riders now had stirrups, but otherwise they were still equipped just as the Wikosans would be. It had been bittersweet as well as amusing for Benton to see that the Asterans had carefully copied the cavalry stirrups right down to the "U.S." embossed on the leather.

"Are you all right?" Benton asked Tyndall, knowing that Belisa was with that mounted force.

"I think so, cap'n. But when we parted, Belisa said she hoped I'd come home with an enemy's head tied to my saddle. Do you think she meant that?"

He hadn't seen any signs of such primitive, bloodthirsty behavior among the Asterans. "It sounds like a traditional thing to say to someone going off to fight. Something from their ancient past that isn't meant literally anymore."

The sergeant nodded, his brow furrowed in thought. "I expect you're right, sir. Or, at least I hope you're right. I do like Belisa, cap'n, but there's some things I draw the line at doing even when a woman asks me."

Scouts searching with extreme care well off to either side of the road had confirmed the suspicions of the Asterans and the cavalry. There were mounted forces moving on both the north and the south sides of the road, far enough away to be unseen by anyone watching the Wikosan infantry march up the road itself. Wikosan scouts coming down the road had sighted the advancing Asteran infantry and raced back to tell their commanders.

Benton led his cavalry overland, moving as quietly as possible, using any cover available, traveling far enough to the south to outflank the Wikosan mounted force planning to outflank the Asterans on the road. Much farther to the north, Odwan Freya was leading a force of Asteran infantry and the small Asteran mounted force to outflank the Wikosans on the north side.

The Wikosans appeared to have at least six hundred mounted fighters, against the combined numbers of a US Cavalry and Asteran mounted force of less than one hundred fifty. Little wonder the Wikosans advanced with too much confidence and too little care, trusting in their deception and their strong superiority in numbers.

The final approach to the battlefield was in the predawn dimness, the cavalry column moving silently through prairie grass dry and brown from the winter. The wagons had been left behind in the city, unneeded for such a short period in the field, and too likely to be spotted by the enemy. As the sun rose, Captain Benton led his company through small, unnamed courses and creek beds south of Dry Creek. "Lieutenant Garret."

"Yes, sir."

"We're leading our horses to conserve their strength. Did your professors teach you the other reason for walking horses rather than riding them?"

"No, sir."

Benton pointed upward. "A man on a horse has a much higher silhouette than a man and a horse walking. A man riding a horse can be seen by a man on the ground much farther than they can see that man."

Reaching their objective, Benton halted the column and pulled out his field glasses, then handed his horse's reins to the bugler and hiked up the side of the gulley they were in to look north, keeping low as he reached the top. He gazed through the field glasses, slowly traversing the landscape, but from here couldn't see the main Wikosan force coming up the road, or the Asterans coming up to meet them. There was no sign of the left or right hook of the Wikosans, either, or of Freya's force farther north. "Lieutenant Garret, go back west along this gulley and see if you can spot any of the moving forces. Sergeant Tyndall, get our own scouts out to the north and see what they can find."

Benton lowered his field glasses, unhappy at his inability to communicate with the other parts of the Asteran force but knowing there was nothing he could do about it. The people of this world knew all about using mirrors to flash simple messages quickly over long distances. Indeed, the ruined imperial guard towers they'd seen had done that as part of their mission. But attempting to flash messages between the different parts of the Asteran force now would only betray their presence to any Wikosans moving in the same line of sight.

As the sun climbed in the sky it beat down into the gulley, the air growing warm despite the season. Down here, the almost ever-present Kansas wind couldn't penetrate well, so the cavalry sat and literally sweated out the wait, most of the cavalrymen grabbing a nap with the practiced efficiency of veterans.

Lieutenant Garret finally came back, moving bent over to keep from being seen by any Wikosan looking this way, and knelt beside Benton. "Captain, the Asterans are coming up the road just as planned. They and the Wikosans on the road are in sight of each other and both sides are spreading out on either side of the road for a fight."

Several minutes later three of Benton's scouts scuttled out of the grass and slid into the gulley. "Sir, them Wickies are there in Dry Creek, all right. About five hundred yards north of here. All cavalry, near as we could tell," Corporal Stein reported. "About three company's worth of them, I figure."

Roughly three hundred, then. "Do they have any scouts out on this side?"

"No, sir. Not a one. And all of them are looking north toward the road. I reckon we could've walked up and carried off a couple of them and the rest wouldn't have noticed."

"Show me where they are." The scouts pointed, Benton studying the area carefully through his field glasses and now spotting a few plumes among trees growing in the creek bed. Some careless Wikosans were wearing helmets that stood up high enough to see. "Is there anything for the horses to worry about between us and them?"

Corporal Stein pointed east. "A little prairie dog town over that way, captain. That's it."

"Good job. Lieutenant Garret, let's get the company lined up."

They'd learned all about this from the plains tribes. How to sneak up on an enemy, ensuring surprise, the importance of scouting the terrain carefully, and then an overwhelming attack before those being assaulted had time to gather their wits.

Moving with care to avoid making noise, the company formed into one line facing toward the enemy, each cavalryman holding his horse and ready to mount, about one yard between the men and horses as they stood abreast. "Pass the word down the line," Benton ordered. "The men are to use their pistols. They are to fire a volley just before contact with the enemy, and only after emptying their pistols are they to draw sabers and fight with blades."

Sergeant Tyndall passed the word, then grinned at Benton. "Good thing you got the company some of them new Smith and Wesson revolvers, cap'n."

Good thing, indeed, given the odds facing them. The .44 caliber Smith and Wessons that the Army had bought this year could fire six shots almost as fast as a trooper could pull the trigger, whereas the old Model 1860 Colt cap and ball pistols had taken a while to fire each shot and a long time to reload.

Then they could only wait. Benton kept looking north, but his thoughts were often not on the Wikosans, but on the Asteran force to the north commanded by Odwan Freya.

"They'll be fine, cap'n," Sergeant Tyndall startled him by saying in a low voice. "Belisa says that Odwan is one tough fighter."

"Thanks," Benton muttered, embarrassed that Tyndall had read his feelings.

A moment later, the sounds of horns floated over the prairie. "Those are ours, cap'n," Tyndall confirmed. "Asteran, I mean. They're ordering the infantry on the road to advance."

The feint attack was going in. "Pass the word for the men to prepare to mount," Benton ordered.

Tyndall took a long drink from his canteen, then spat to one side. "Faking a retreat is hard to do right, cap'n. You think that Agani and Costoni can do it?"

"They've got the best troops the Asterans can muster as well as the worst, and the best ones are supposed to form a shield wall in the rear to keep the weaker ones from really running." That was how it was supposed to work, anyway.

More Asteran horns, Tyndall listening carefully. "That's the order to attack, cap'n."

"Mount up."

All along the line, cavalrymen swung into their saddles, one hand grasping their bridles and the other drawing and cocking their pistols.

"Uncase the colors."

The flag of the United States of America and the guidon of the 5th Cavalry regiment came free of their canvas tubes, unfurling in the breeze.

The sounds of the horns were confused now. Decires Agani and Costoni had command of the force on the road, which was even weaker than it appeared since half of it was made up of the sort of older, younger or inexperienced fighters whom Freya had characterized as only good enough to defend the walls. Those soldiers would be falling back now as the Wikosans advanced, the enemy no doubt thrilled at how easily the Asteran attack seemed to be crumbling.

Benton raised one hand. "Company B, advance at a walk!" His hand came down and the cavalry surged into a walk, moving as one, the line of men and horses coming up from the gully and heading toward the still-hidden mounted force of Wikosans. Dressing their line to keep it as straight as possible, the company advanced.

This was the hard part for any cavalry force, to wait to commence the charge until they were the right distance from the enemy. Charge too early, and the horses would be spent when they made contact. Charge too late, and they might not have enough speed up.

The metal-on-metal clanging din of battle on the road could be heard now as well as the calls of horns, and Benton saw the Wikosan mounted force, still screened from the road but every man in their own saddles now, every head turned north toward the fight.

Three hundred yards, the cavalry moving steadily through the high prairie grass, silent but for the rattle of harness and the crackling of the dry grass being shoved aside by the horses. Two hundred yards, the Wikosans milling about, plainly eager to go but waiting for some signal.

"Bugler," Benton ordered. "Sound the trot."

As the notes of the bugle rose over the prairie, the line of cavalry kicked their horses into a trot.

The enemy horsemen looked back as the sounds of the bugle finally rose over the racket of the nearby battle and the noise of the Wikosans' own horses and gear. Their mouths gaped open in shock, then Benton heard them shouting warnings to each other.

One hundred and fifty yards. "Bugler, sound the gallop."

This time the bugle call was more insistent, and at the demand of their riders the cavalry horses leaped forward, the straight line maintaining its order even as the horses raced faster toward the enemy. Benton gripped his pistol harder, the wind whipping at his face.

The Wikosans were turning their horses and colliding with each other as the enemy force struggled to reorient toward the new threat.

Roughly fifty yards. "Bugler, sound the charge!" Benton shouted over the thunder of one hundred horses galloping to the attack. The bugle sang urgently and continuously, its notes ringing over the battlefield, and now the cavalrymen roared as they kicked their horses into an all-out assault, the flags flying open behind the color bearers as Company B hit the enemy with the mass and momentum only a cavalry charge could create.

Benton leveled his pistol at a Wikosan who seemed to be shouting orders, firing a few feet short of contact with the enemy, other pistols going off all along the line as the rest of the troopers fired. The Wikosans, already wavering, broke frantically toward the road, all thought of attacking fled as the cavalry herded them north, firing and shouting, the Wikosan horses panicking at the noise again and throwing many of those riders who weren't being felled by the .44 caliber bullets from the revolvers which punched easily through the armor of the Wikosans.

He could see the road now, the Asteran force holding a blocking position along the road to the west while the Wikosan infantry pressed forward against it. But the sound of the gunshots from the cavalry had already alerted the Wikosans on the road to their peril, and Benton saw them beginning to fall back. He shot another Wikosan at point blank range, the impact of the shot knocking the enemy out of the saddle, then took two more shots to drop a Wikosan with a lance. His next bullet went into a dismounted Wikosan who was staggering around waving a axe.

The cavalry was near the road now, herding the surviving Wikosan horsemen toward their infantry, the horns of the Asterans on the road sounding as their holding action turned into a slow, steady advance. The Asteran line thinned, extending outward to either side to curl around the edges of the Wikosan infantry formation as the Wikosans fell back.

From the north, more Wikosans came, riding frantically, then hauling in their reins as they saw the cavalry charging up from the south, pistol shots still crashing over the lesser sounds of swords on shields or armor. The small Asteran mounted force appeared just north of the road beyond the Wikosans there, the blue banner spangled with stars identifying them clearly as they blocked the road, then Asteran infantry came into view to the north, advancing quickly in line, shields locked, pressing the northern hook into the Wikosan infantry on the road where the fleeing remnants of the southern hook were already stampeding into their own infantry.

Benton wheeled his formation, forcing the Wikosans ahead of him to crash into the Wikosan infantry as they tried to escape. The enemy mounted force which had formed the northern hook was mostly intact since it had been able to outrun the Asteran infantry, but it was also forced into its own infantry as it tried to flee and the Wikosan force was pressed on all sides. The cavalry wheeled again and Asteran infantry pushed forward and around, the forces on the road moving to link up with the northern advance as it reached the road behind the Wikosans. The Asteran mounted soldiers charged into a band of fleeing Wikosan mounted men who seemed about to escape, driving those Wikosans back upon their infantry as well.

A line of Wikosan infantry headed for the last open escape path, moving southeast with their shields joined to form a solid defense.

Benton slowed his horse, turning to shout at the thirty or so cavalrymen closest to him. "Carbines!" The cavalrymen checked their mounts, drawing their carbines and aiming at the escaping Wikosans. Shooting from the saddle was notoriously inaccurate, but the wall of Wikosans was almost impossible to miss. "Fire!" A ragged volley erupted from the carbines, and several of the Wikosans in the front rank were punched backwards by hits. The rest of the escaping Wikosans hesitated, stumbling to a halt.

Sergeant Tyndall led another group of cavalry close to the Wikosans, reining in their horses only twenty feet from the infantry and firing their carbines in a devastating salvo.

The Wikosan infantry broke, running back towards their comrades, smashing into other Wikosans who had tried to follow them out of the trap.

The southern flank of the Asteran infantry under Agani and Costoni made contact with the southern edge of the Asteran infantry which had come from the north, closing the net and completely encircling the Wikosans.

The Wikosans on each side of the formation tried to force their way to the other side to escape, only to discover an unbroken line of Asterans on all sides. The enemy army turned into a mob as panic set in and the vengeful Asterans locked shields and pressed in harder, an unyielding wall of armor and weapons ringing in the Wikosans who were increasingly packed too tightly to fight well and were no longer offering any effective resistance.

"Bugler, sound assembly." Benton's mount was exhausted, almost staggering as he reined the horse to a walk. This was the infantry's battle now. The surviving Wikosan mounted forces were trapped in the heaving mass of foot soldiers, their horses lashing out at their own side in panic.

He looked down at the saber in his hand. He couldn't clearly remember holstering his empty pistol and drawing the saber, but the blade had a slick of blood on the edge where he had struck a Wikosan.

Lieutenant Garret rode up, his face pale but his eyes still lit from the excitement of battle. "Two dead, six wounded, sir. Four horses down."

"Thank you, lieutenant." Benton, trying to keep his hands from trembling, carefully wiped his saber blade and returned the weapon to its scabbard. "Who are the dead?"

"Private Murphy and Private Frost, sir."

"Damn. Sergeant Tyndall, check on the wounded, let me know how serious their injuries are, and make sure the Asteran surgeons know we have wounded who need treating."

Tyndall saluted and rushed off at the best pace his winded horse could manage.

Lieutenant Garret stared toward where the Asteran infantry was still crushing the helpless rabble which had been the Wikosan army. "As close to another Cannae as matters, captain."

"Yes, lieutenant. Congratulations on your first battle. You handled yourself well." Benton sighed, looking back at the fight before kicking his reluctant horse into motion again. "The Wikosans don't stand a chance now, but they keep trying to fight. The Asterans don't need us to assist in the slaughter. Let's see to our dead."

Corporal O'Hare was standing sentry with the bodies, his face stiff with grief, and saluted as Benton approached. "Beg to report, captain, that Private Murphy and Private Frost are dead."

"I heard." Benton dismounted and knelt by the bodies. The dead soldiers had already been laid out properly, their eyes closed. "They were good men."

"Yes, sir. Captain, sir, how do we bury them, sir?" O'Hare seemed very agitated as he asked the question.

"Like any soldier, corporal. A sad duty, but it's one we've carried out before this. Why do you ask?"

"Captain, sir, it's −" O'Hare waved a hand to encompass their surroundings. "I haven't seen a church here, sir. Not one. And not one man of God, neither. The city folk are nice and all, but they've never heard of Him. How can we give our men a proper burial if… if the Lord's not here to accept them?"

Benton stood up, raising one hand to clasp O'Hare's shoulder. "Corporal, were you taught that He is everywhere?"

"Yes, sir. That I was."

"Then He is here, corporal. We will bury our men as they would have wished to be buried, with the full regulation service, and He will take their souls in His hand, because He is here with us."

O'Hare's face cleared, anxiety being replaced by a relieved smile. "Of course, sir. I knew I should ask you right off, captain. Yes, sir. At the city, sir? We'll bury them there? The city folk won't mind the crosses on the grave markers, will they?"

"No, corporal, the Asterans won't mind."

As Benton mounted again, Lieutenant Garret came to stand by his stirrup. "Captain, that thing you told the corporal," Garret asked quietly. "Do you believe it?"

Benton leaned forward, looking down at Garret, "Lieutenant, during the war the 5th Cavalry fought in a lot of battles. The Wilderness was one of them. It was also the nearest thing to hell I ever hope to experience. During the Wilderness, I thought the only way I could possibly live through the fight would be if the Lord stayed right beside me. As you see, I did survive the battle. If the Lord could be with me through that, I'm sure He's here, too."

"But what if our world is still there somehow, if both it and this world exist at the same time?"

"If General Grant could handle more than one division, I reckon the Lord can handle more than one world, lieutenant. Make sure O'Hare has all the help he needs to get Private Murphy's and Private Frosts' remains prepared for the ride to Astera."

Wearily, Benton rode back toward the fight. The massacre seemed to have stopped, and now the Asterans were holding under guard about two hundred Wikosans who had finally surrendered rather than fight to the death. Benton guessed that something on the order of fifteen hundred Wikosans lay dead on the field.

He spotted Freya riding toward him, a trickle of blood welling from a long cut on one side of her somber face, and Benton's breath caught for a moment. Freya was wearing the same battle gear as when he had first seen her, and though the rents in the chain mail then had since been repaired, there were new gashes in the mail from today's fight. *Thank heavens she's all right. What a woman, to conceive and win such a battle as this. No. All I need say is what a woman. I don't need to add more than that.*

Freya reined in next to him and gave Benton an Asteran salute. "My friend and ally. Thank you. This could not have happened without your cavalry. The mounted forces facing us fled when they heard your weapons. I thank the Light that you have survived and brought home the head of an enemy."

There seemed to be a lot of emotion behind Freya's words. Wondering if that was just because of the passions generated by the battle, Benton looked away, and found himself gazing toward the surviving Wikosans, who were staring back at him with dread and despair. "What's going to happen to them?"

Freya shrugged. "They laid down their arms rather than die holding their place, so they belong to us now, and there's much work to be done in and around Astera."

It took him a moment to realize what she meant. "They're going to be enslaved?"

"Made to work, yes, as long as they live. They are ours." She must have noticed his reaction. "What is wrong, my friend?"

He took a deep breath before speaking, wondering if the promising alliance with Astera was about to founder at the moment of its greatest success, and whether his friendship with Freya would also wither. "I have told you of the war my country fought only a few years ago. In just one battle of that war more than six thousand men died and tens of thousands more were wounded. We fought that war to save the Union, but also to eliminate the stain of slavery from our nation. Our Odwan then, a wise man named Lincoln, said 'as I would not be a slave, so I would not be a master.' My company will not fight to enslave others, Odwan Freya. To do so would be to betray our comrades who died in that war and to betray the beliefs we hold that slavery is always an evil and a wrong."

Freya listened without interrupting, her eyes on his, and remained silent for a long while after Benton finished. "Did you fight in that war?" she finally asked.

"I did, Odwan Freya. So did Sergeant Tyndall and some other members of my troop."

"It is well you survived that, too." Turning her horse, Freya rode a short distance until she was right next to the huddled prisoners. Rising in her new stirrups, she addressed the Wikosans, using only those words of her language which she knew Benton could understand. "Choose twelve among you to return to Wikosa. You will tell Wikosa that they may buy your lives and your freedom with any Asterans they hold, and with horses, cattle, sheep, grain, gold and other metals. What Wikosa has taken will be returned to us, and more besides if they wish you back whole."

She rode back to Benton, ignoring surprised looks from the other Asterans. "Wikosa will pay. It will need them to defend itself when the wolves come to howl at its walls. My people will accept this when they see it profits us. Is this well?" she asked. "Would your Odwan Lincoln approve?"

"He would. Thank you, Odwan Freya."

"Thank you for frank words which ring true. You must tell me more of this Odwan Lincoln. I once said your civilization was backward in some ways, but it seems we can learn from yours just as you have learned from ours."

It turned out that there had been one decire of mounted fighters from Lacanan among the Wikosan army, but they had been completely wiped out in the battle, with none to bring home the tale of their defeat. Freya assigned a messenger to bring the news to Lacanan, along with an offer of alliance which would have been scorned before, but in the wake of this battle would surely receive serious consideration.

In the week after the victorious forces returned to Astera, a Telasan force seven decires strong was spotted marching north, but turned back when brought news of the Wikosan defeat. One of the wounded cavalrymen had suffered such serious injuries to one arm that Benton feared he would have to lose the limb, but the Asteran surgeons worked on it and applied their salves and treatments, afterwards declaring that both man and arm should recover fully. Private Murphy and Private Frost were buried with full military honors, the poignant notes of Taps sounding in the city for the first time for that purpose. Construction began on the powder mill, even though Astera was still trying to secure a reliable source of sulfur. Three more cavalrymen married local girls, and the grateful Asteran city council agreed to formalize the regular payment of salaries to the cavalry so Benton could once again be sure of routinely being able to pay his men. He was especially pleased that the pay rate the Asterans agreed to was equivalent to at least twenty dollars a month for the privates.

On the seventh night after returning, Benton walked out onto the walls surrounding the city, looking west toward where the lights of Fort Harker and Ellsworth, Kansas had been, should have been, but in this world had never been.

"Something troubles you." Freya had come near and now spoke quietly.

"There's someplace I should have gone, Freya, someplace I should have returned my company. But I failed in that."

"Failed? I do not believe you could have failed."

Benton smiled bitterly. "I'm a fairly good officer, I think, but not outstanding. No one would ever confuse me with Sheridan or Sherman."

"More of your Odwans?'

"No, just war leaders."

Freya waited a moment to see if Benton had more to say before she spoke again. "You are better than you believe, I think. Your men seem happy."

"Most of them, yes. Most of them believe we're still going to get home someday, and in the meantime this is as nice a posting as any cavalryman can hope for. Most of the men in the company didn't have a wife or a steady girlfriend back home," Benton explained. "A few do, though, and that's a hard thing, to know you may never see them again."

Freya paused, then spoke carefully. "Do you have such a woman, Captain Benton?"

He didn't answer for a moment, decided to only reply in the negative as he usually did when someone asked that, then found himself saying much more. "No. My wife died several years ago, during the war with the South. It's…not easy to think of even now, because when I left for the war she was so worried that I wouldn't return, that I'd never be able to come back to her. But while I was campaigning she fell ill and died, so when I came home she couldn't be there. I…can't think of it without hoping she didn't know her last hours were her last, because it would have hurt her so to know she wouldn't be there waiting for me when I came back." Benton couldn't recall the last time he'd spoken of that to anyone.

Freya regarded him gravely. "May the Light ease the burden of your grief and the stars shine in memory of the one you have lost." The words sounded ritualistic, but she said them with real feeling.

"Thank you. What about you, Odwan Freya?"

She made a sad sound. "I had a man who died nearly half my life ago, in battle. He stays young in my memory. Now I am bound to my duty as Odwan. There has been little room for anyone else. You understand?"

"Yes, I do. I'm sorry for your loss. I'm grateful there is room in your life for my friendship." It felt both comfortable and strange to be speaking so with a woman, one who truly did share so many things with him, who also knew how the burdens of command could force out personal wants and needs. The only thing standing between them like a wall was a truth which Benton hadn't yet shared with her. "I need to tell you where we actually came from, Freya."

She shook her head. "Whatever led you from there is nothing I need know."

"Yes, I think you do." He explained his world, the storm, the changed world they'd found afterwards, and Lieutenant Garret's theory. "We have no idea how to get back, but if we ever found a way, we'd have to use it. I have a duty to fulfill."

To his surprise, Freya didn't express any disbelief, instead nodding knowingly. "The lightning. Its ancient name is the fire-writer, that which the Light uses to cast messages in the sky, messages whose meaning we often cannot read. The lightning brought you here from the world you knew, but the reason may never be clear." She sighed. "Your cavalry has saved Astera not once but twice and guaranteed our safety for years to come. You have already done so much. Yet, you may also help us and other cities build peace in this part of the land again, the type of peace no one has seen since the days of the fallen empire. But our debt and our duty is clear. If Astera, if I, can ever help you reach your home again, we will. But the lightning never repeats the same message twice."

"We say much the same thing," Benton replied, turning away from the darkness where his duty had lain, turning to face Freya.

She smiled and touched his face gently with one hand. "No matter what the lightning does, you will always have a home here."

POSTSCRIPT

Though historical memory of the Benton Massacre has been eclipsed by the Fetterman Disaster in 1866 and Custer's Last Stand at the Little Big Horn in 1876, it attracted considerable attention for a brief period and remains an enduring military mystery. On October 4th, 1870, a company from the 5th Cavalry Regiment under the command of Captain Ulysses Benton left Fort Harker on a routine training patrol of the area south and west of the fort in preparation for campaigning later in the season. The company of cavalry did not return as scheduled, and every attempt to locate Captain Benton or any of his men failed. Nearby tribes all denied knowing what had happened to the cavalry unit, but an official investigation concluded that the only plausible explanation for their disappearance had to be a massacre of the entire company and the concealment of their bodies and equipment. No trace of Captain Benton's command has ever been found.

AUTHOR'S NOTE
FAILURE TO OBEY

My second series of books featured the exploits of a new officer in the space Navy who has the misfortune to be appointed the legal officer on his first ship. While handling all of the other duties of a shipboard officer, Paul Sinclair also has to give his commanding officer advice on legal matters based on a four-week-long school. (Yes, the Navy does that kind of thing to you. The Navy did that to me.) After four books, Paul's saga went into temporary hibernation while I worked on the Lost Fleet story, but people kept asking what happened after the end of that fourth book. One of my own real jobs in the US Navy had involved anti-terrorism, so I had learned a lot about how terrorists work. However, I couldn't use that knowledge in stories because I didn't want any real terrorists getting any good tips from whatever scenario I used. It finally occurred to me that I could set a terrorist attack on a space station, using a method of attack that wouldn't work on Earth, and tell a story about that. And one of the main settings in the Sinclair books was a US Navy space station. Paul had been sent off to Mars at the end of book four, but I still had his partner Lieutenant Jen Shen on that space station, as well as Paul's old Master-at-Arms Ivan Sharpe. This is what happened to them.

FAILURE TO OBEY

Perhaps it was some instinct born of experience that made Lieutenant Jen Shen jerk awake in the middle of the night, the voices of dead shipmates echoing in her fading dreams, and lunge for the survival suit kept in a ready locker right next to her bunk. She was halfway into the suit before the structure of Benjamin Franklin Naval Space Station shuddered twice, and fastening the last seals before the blare of the general quarters alarm began resounding urgently.

No one was in sight as Jen slammed shut the door to the closet-sized room that made up her personal quarters and began pelting down the passageway toward main engineering control. Heading in toward the hollow center of the vast rotating disc which was Franklin, Jen was going uphill against the rotation-induced gravity, taking ladders two steps at a time as she tried to cover ground before airtight hatches closed and made progress much slower. As she approached the armored survival bulkhead between her and engineering control, the massive hatch at the end of the passageway began sliding shut as its own warning alert added to the clamor. Jen managed to slide through sideways just in time, feeling the station jerk several times again as unknown forces slammed the structure.

Another ladder up, then another hatch loomed before her, this one sealed tight. She rammed her palm against the reader next to the hatch, punching the "open" button repeatedly as Jen waited for the reader to identify her from the chip embedded in her hand.

The hatch swung open, Jen hurled herself inside, and the hatch slammed behind her. It took two more passageways, ladders and hatches before she reached her objective.

She finally paused, then, to take in the scene in main engineering control. At this hour, only the watch standers were present, five enlisted sailors led by Chief Petty Officer Carreras, all of whom were already in survival suits as well. "What's going on?" Jen demanded.

Carreras looked at her, his expression impossible to read through the face plate of his suit. "Damned if I know, lieutenant. We've got system failures cascading through part of the station inboard from here and it feels like there's explosions in that area, but the sensors are dead. We've all been ordered to stay here while command central tries to find out what's going on."

Typical. Too many people depended on remote sensors for information and didn't know what to do if those sensors failed. Eventually command central would order investigators into the area, but experience had proven to Jen just how critical time was in responding to emergencies. "I haven't been ordered to stay here." Fighting off a flashback to the devastating explosion on her old ship the *Maury*, Jen punched open the hatch leading toward the affected areas.

She ran again, up a ladder and down the narrow passageway leading to the area of the station where supplies and the water tanks were warehoused near the hollow core, yanking open the hatch at the far end. Once again, some instinct made her pause before dashing through, and she saw two figures in survival suits moving toward her from the damaged area. Wind whistled past, warning of breaches in the hull where atmosphere was venting. "What's –" she started to ask them.

Both of the figures raised weapons and began running toward her. Jen just stared in disbelief for a moment, then slammed her fist onto the "close" button as one of the figures opened fire, metal slugs rattling off of the closing hatch in a deafening hail. Punching in a code, she locked the hatch against anyone without the proper access. She had a sinking suspicion that anyone who had blown their way inside the station could also get through interior hatches, but it might slow down whoever the attackers were.

This time Jen ran even faster, half-sliding/half-falling down the ladder and reaching the hatch to engineering central as Franklin's structure shuddered again. Looking back, she saw the hatch she'd sealed falling inward, its edges glowing with intense heat, figures in survival suits coming through quickly, all carrying weapons.

Jen sealed and locked this hatch, too, calling out orders to the watch standers in engineering central. "We're under attack! Notify command central! It's people wearing survival suits like ours. Numbers unknown." As a stunned Chief Carreras called command central, Jen rushed to one of the control consoles. "Shut everything down! Shift all controls to secondary stations! Do it now! Those guys are right behind me!"

The enlisted hesitated only a second, then frantically began following Jen's orders. As Jen worked, she heard command central's response to the chief's message. "Understood. Presence of armed attackers inside the station is confirmed. We're deploying the emergency response teams to counter them."

Despite her urgency, Jen spun to glare at the screen. "Masters-at-arms carrying light weapons? This isn't a riot, central! These guys are heavily armed!"

The commander on the screen visibly wavered. Jen understood why. Over-reaction would make him look ridiculous, and nobody wanted to admit they couldn't handle a situation on their own. But she knew they'd need help. "*Belleau Wood* is inport, right? She's got Marines aboard. Call them out."

"Marines?"The commander hesitated again. As he did so, a series of shudders rolled through the space station's structure, making everyone waver on their feet, followed by an odd groaning sound from the metal and composites making up the station, a noise which made Jen's hair stand on end. The sensation of gravity wobbled erratically. That seemed to make up the commander's mind. "Yes. Marines."

"The attackers are heading this way and can blow through hatches. We're shutting everything down and evacuating now." As her console and the comm screen went dark, Jen glanced at the locked hatch, seeing the edges starting to glow. "Get out! Everybody out! I'm right behind you, Chief."

The enlisted watch standers bolted toward the hatch that Jen had originally entered through as Jen ran from console to console to confirm they were shutting down. She paused for a moment at one, viciously punching a confirm command on one console which hadn't accepted its shut down orders yet, then leaped toward the safe hatch as the glowing hatch failed and fell inward.

Chief Carreras and the others pulled her through, slamming the hatch shut behind Jen. Metal slugs impacted against the closing hatch and the bulkhead around it, then the hatch sealed and locked. Everyone paused for a moment, staring at each other. "They going to come through here?" one of the watch standers asked.

"They wanted engineering central," Carreras answered, looking to Jen for confirmation.

"Yeah."With all control systems active, anyone in charge of engineering central could have caused havoc throughout the station before control could be remotely switched to secondary systems. "It won't do them much good now, though. How the hell did they get inside the station?"

Another enlisted had broken open the damage control locker in this compartment and was hefting a pry bar. "Maybe we can stop them from getting any farther."

"We can try," Jen agreed. Pry bars and other damage control tools against slug throwers was crazy, but they might have a chance as the attackers came through the hatch. "Get into position on either side of the hatch while I call command central."

The comm screen here cleared to reveal a captain this time, who was staring from display to display in the command central compartment as the commander they'd seen earlier spoke quickly to him. "They've taken engineering central," Jen reported. "We'll try to hold them here."

The captain nodded jerkily, his eyes on the displays. "Confirm all system controls were shifted to secondary control stations."

"Affirmative."

"Good work. The masters-at-arms are engaging the attackers and the Marines are on their way. Retaking engineering central will be a high-priority task for the Marines. Stand by for them and let us know if the attackers try to come through where you are now."

"Understood. Stand by, hold position and wait for Marines." Jen slumped for a moment as the screen blanked, swallowing to moisten a mouth dry from recent events. But she was in command here, with no time for letting the situation get to her. She turned toward the enlisted. "You guys heard? We hold here."

The petty officer with the pry bar hefted it, smiling in a way that betrayed fear as well as determination. "We'll damn well try, ma'am."

They waited for minutes which seemed to drag for hours. The station trembled and vibrated at odd intervals, the majestic rotation of its huge mass being affected by whatever the attackers were doing. Occasionally they could feel gravity oscillate as if they were riding a roller coaster. Jen thought about the ships mated to the berths lining the top and bottom of the station's disc, wondering if they were executing emergency breakaways to keep themselves safe, or staying attached to the station to keep its mass distribution from fluctuating even worse than it obviously already was.

The hatch behind them shot open with shocking suddenness and Marines boiled into the compartment. Jen stared at them. She'd seen Marines in combat armor before, suits whose bulk and strength far surpassed the survival suits worn by sailors, but now Jen fully understood just how menacing those Marines could be on full combat footing, their weapons questing for targets.

One of the Marines focused on her. "Lieutenant Shen? I'm Lieutenant Yohl. They're on the other side of that hatch?"

"They were," Jen confirmed.

"Is the equipment in there hardened?"

"Against radiation? Yeah. There's back-up circuits running through vacuum tubes. Extremely limited capabilities reducing our read-outs to blinking lights and a few plain text messages on a CRT."

"CRT?"

"Cathode ray tube. Really primitive video. The back-up circuits require humans in the loop, but they'll work for the most basic functions once we do restarts. Anyway, right now everything is routed to redundant secondary control locations scattered through other parts of the station. If the station loses one of those or connectivity to one of them, then we'll have to run part of things through the back-ups in there. It won't be pretty, but we can do it." They trained for working with minimal automated support, scrolling text reporting basic data, ancient circuitry designs getting the necessary information to human brains making decisions and inputting commands, trying to substitute their own training, experience and intuition for the precise, lightning fast calculations of modern circuitry. It did work. In an ugly, headache-and-sweat inducing, close-enough-for-government-work way. People had first gone to the moon using that kind of computing power, the training manuals said. Or, as the saying went, "it was good enough for Apollo, wasn't it?" In popular use that saying usually ended up being sarcastic, though, and applied to everything from food quality to the amount of area in living accommodations.

None of that mattered to the Marine, of course. All he cared about was that Jen had said the Navy could live without those circuits for a while. "Okay. Get your people away from the hatch, ma'am."

Jen gathered her sailors in the far corner of the compartment, watching as the Marines resealed the hatch they'd entered through and then prepared to retake engineering central. "Fire in the hole," she heard someone warn, and lowered her head to shield herself. A dull thump echoed through the compartment, then Jen raised her eyes to see the hatch blowing in towards engineering central in several large fragments. To her surprise, no atmosphere vented behind the hatch, revealing that the spaces beyond weren't in vacuum. She was still wincing at the thought of what those hatch fragments might do to the equipment inside when one of the Marines fired a stubby weapon through the ruined hatch, then huddled back.

Jen's survival suited blared warnings as it picked up the edges of the electro-magnetic pulse the Marines had detonated inside engineering central. She heard Chief Carreras's sigh, and knew he was thinking about all of the transistors, integrated circuits and processor arrays which had just been fried by that EMP burst. But at least the vacuum tubes would have been unaffected by it, and any electrical systems on the attackers or their weapons would have been fried as well.

The Marines stormed through the hatch, firing as they went. Jen couldn't tell how many shots the attackers got off, but after a couple of minutes a Marine reappeared and waved her forward. "Ma'am, we've secured this compartment."

Jen brought the sailors with her back into engineering central, fighting down a gust of despair as she saw the damage inside. Three figures in survival suits lay splayed about the compartment, the suits marred by charred holes where Marine rounds had punched through. The Marines were already moving down the passageway as

Jen directed the watch standers to assess the damage. She tried to ignore the dead attackers, focusing resolutely on her job.

A hand on her shoulder shocked her. Jen jumped back to see more figures in survival suits, these unarmed. "Easy, Jen. It's Bob Nuevos."

"Nice seeing you, commander." Jen got control of herself, waving around the compartment. "It's a mess."

"Yeah. Listen, I've been ordered to take charge here until Captain Dila arrives. The sensor grids inside the damaged parts of the station have been blown to hell. We have to know what the damage is like in there."

And you want me to volunteer. "There's still fighting going on, and the bad guys are wearing survival suits that look like ours."

"You'll have a Marine escort."

So much for that excuse. "Fine. I'll go."

"Run a comm line behind you so we can receive your reports. There's no telling how badly damaged the comm relays are inside that area."

"Got it." Jen paused. "I don't know why there's atmosphere in here. I know there was venting going on when I first sighted the attackers. Maybe from breaches they blew to get inside the station. But they must have sealed any holes in the outer structure after that."

Commander Nuevos didn't answer for a moment. "That's odd. They wouldn't need atmosphere since they're wearing survival suits and vacuum would've complicated our repair efforts. See if you can find out why they restored airtight integrity."

"Aye, aye, sir." She wouldn't explain the true reason for her reluctance, wouldn't admit that the idea of struggling through wrecked compartments made her break into a cold sweat as images of the damage done to *Maury* came back to her.

Two Marines waited just outside of engineering central, somehow conveying by their postures how unhappy they were at being saddled with escorting a Navy officer instead of being on the front lines of the fight. "Let's go," Jen ordered.

She hadn't made it to the ladder leading up to the next hatch when she realized water was trickling down the ladder and pooling beneath it. Looking up, Jen saw water splashing over the coaming of the hatch the attackers had blown. At least one of the pressurized water tanks serving Franklin had been breeched.

Stepping through the hatch, Jen tried to survey the damage, seeing holes blown in bulkheads and walls at floor level. As she moved forward, the water grew deeper, then shallower, as if it were rolling back and forth inside the damaged area. Jen tried to assess how much water was involved, then staggered as a particularly high surge swirled up above her shins. At the same time, she heard another one of those eerie groans from the structure of the station. "Oh my God."

"Lieutenant?" one of the Marines asked.

"I just figured out what's going on." She keyed the circuit back to engineering central. "Commander Nuevos!"

"This is Captain Dila. What'd you find, lieutenant?"

"A lot of water and passages blown for it to move freely in these spaces, captain. They blew at least two main water tanks, and it's surging back and forth already."

"Surging?"

Jen remembered that Captain Dila didn't have much shipboard experience back on Earth. "Free surface effect, captain. If we don't get this water pumped and corralled it'll keep picking up energy and magnifying its force as it rushes back and forth in here."

Dila might not have served on many ships, but he was a good engineer. "That amount of mass running free? It could tear this entire section of the station apart."

"Yes, sir. We need pumps rigged to secure the water and we need damage control teams to seal the holes that are letting the water move about, and we need them half an hour ago."

She heard Dila issuing orders, then his voice came back clearly to her. "Lieutenant Shen, where exactly are you now?"

"Passageway Seven Alpha Frame Ninety-two."

"Is there any fighting in the area?"

"No, sir. I can hear fighting but it seems a few compartments away."

"Try to establish how far forward our damage control teams can move to deal with the damage. I'll be sending them in as fast as I can."

Jen exhaled, listening to explosions and shots which already seemed far too close. "Aye, aye, sir." She turned to the Marines. "I need to get as close to the fighting as possible."

Both of the Marines seemed to radiate joy at the chance to get closer to the fight. "Yes, ma'am! Follow us!"

The Marines advanced, crouching down, splashing through the water, their weapons constantly on the move for threats. One of the Marines halted, holding up a warning hand, then slunk forward a meter and examined something on the deck. "Got some fallen sailors here."

Jen pushed forward past the other Marine, who was still standing alert for threats. She knelt in the water, gazing at the two figures in survival suits. Both wore Navy insignia and one still had a sidearm clenched in her fist. Both had been riddled with metal slugs from the attackers' weapons. "Masters-at-arms. They were part of the emergency reaction force." Jacking into their suits, Jen called up the readouts from any systems still functioning. Health status readings were all zero. "They're both dead." Her emotions seemed to have frozen, going back to the day when she had picked her way through the remnants of *Maury*'s engineering spaces and the remnants of the officers and sailors who had been in those spaces.

"They had guts," one of the Marines observed. "Going up against these guys in just those suits and carrying light arms like that."

"Yeah. Let's go."

The sounds of shots came ever closer, punctuated by rolling vibrations in the bulkheads and deck as more explosions rattled the station. Jen caught a glimpse of other Marines, all of them facing in the other direction, then a small detonation echoed through the station's frame and the Marines charged forward, firing. "That's the front line, ma'am," one of her Marines reported.

Jen crouched against a torn bulkhead, holding herself together by sheer willpower. "Captain Dila, I'm at frame forty-one. The fighting is about three meters farther inboard, at frame thirty-eight."

"*Three meters?* Dammit, Shen, get back."

"It's moving away from me, sir." Jen paused as one of her Marine escorts waved for attention.

"Looks like that was the last active resistance, ma'am," the Marine reported. "Our command net is breaking the assault forces into fire teams to search for any attackers lying low." The water rolled up higher around Jen's legs and the station shivered again. "What the hell is that, ma'am?"

"Wave action," she explained. "The Navy's on it." At least, she hoped so. "Captain Dila, my Marines report that active resistance appears to have ceased."

"Thank God. Stay where you are and monitor conditions until the damage control teams reach you. Then I want you to move into the rest of the damaged areas and give us as good a report as you can."

Jen leaned against the bulkhead, listening to and feeling Franklin's structure complain at the unfamiliar stresses, wondering how much progress the damage control teams were making. Finally she heard and then saw a team wading through the passageway toward her, carrying panels which they were hastily tacking into place over the worst holes in the walls to hinder the movement of the water. "Okay, Marines. I've got orders to check out more compartments. You can rejoin your unit."

"Wait, ma'am." The Marine paused to check with his superiors, then somehow shrugged through the combat armor. "We're to stick with you for now, ma'am. The major says we can't afford to lose you."

"It's nice to be appreciated." Jen led the Marines this time, moving into compartments she thought needed to be checked, evaluating damage and calling it back to engineering central so damage control efforts could be prioritized. The water levels were definitely going down now, and the surges back and forth diminishing rapidly in intensity. The noticeable fluctuations in gravity had almost totally ceased. Reaching a bulkhead near the water tanks, Jen frowned down at large holes the attackers had blown near deck level. She crouched to look inside them, confirming that these holes gave onto nothing but a series of spare parts lockers. The identifying information on the bulkheads was up to date as well, but seemed new. She moved several meters to the left, reaching a sturdy bulkhead freshly labeled with warnings in large letters. *Danger. Pressurized Liquid On Other Side Of Bulkhead.* "Why the hell?"

"Ma'am?" one of the Marines asked.

"They blew the holes in the wrong places. If they'd vented this tank, too, they might have wrecked the station. It's impossible to miss these labels. But they blew the wrong bulkhead."

The Marines looked at each other, then one faced Jen again. "Maybe they had orders to blow that bulkhead, ma'am."

"But it was the *wrong* bulkhead."

"It wouldn't be the first time orders were wrong, ma'am. Good thing for us, huh?"

"Yeah. Good thing."

At some point the area was declared clear and the Marines were finally withdrawn back to the *Belleau Wood.* Jen kept up her examination of the damaged areas, sometimes directing damage control teams she came across, until temporary sensor grids were strung in the compartments and she was called back to engineering central. The place was crowded with every available engineer and systems tech, all trying to get full systems capability back online. Fried circuit boards, black boxes and motherboards littered the deck as everyone working on repairs cursed the attackers, the Marines and their motherboarding EMP weapon, and the designers of the control consoles. Jen jumped in on one console, eventually helping get it working at close to one hundred percent again, then volunteered to lead one of the next shift of damage control teams heading into the damaged areas.

No one had yet heard who the attackers were. Aside from the Marines and the surviving masters-at-arms, few had even caught a glimpse of the attackers. "I don't know," Jen kept repeating to everyone who asked her. "I didn't see any identifying markings on them. I'll lay you odds there's nothing on them that ties them to anyone."

At some point in the endless hours of labor, Jen sat down for a moment to eat a ration bar and didn't so much fall asleep as pass out from exhaustion. She was awakened by the sound of her name and bolted upright, staring around in confusion as she tried to shake the fatigue clouding her mind. Focusing, Jen saw a man wearing admiral's stars standing in front of her. But as she tried to spring to attention, the man held out his hands to almost hold her down.

"Relax, lieutenant. You're Shen?"

"Yes, sir." It just felt wrong to sit down while an admiral stood looking at her, but Jen couldn't very well ignore his order to remain seated.

"From all I hear we owe you a great deal, lieutenant. You did one hell of a job, and your quick reactions kept things from being worse. Maybe a lot worse." The admiral gazed soberly at her for a long moment. "Maybe you don't know, but I signed the charge sheet for your court-martial after the accident on the *Maury*. I've made plenty of mistakes in my time, Lieutenant Shen, but today proved that was by far the worst. They teach us never to apologize, but I'm doing it now. I deeply regret what the Navy put you through, and I'll do what I can to make it right. Thank you, lieutenant." The admiral extended his hand and Jen shook it reflexively, feeling even more stunned than before. Then the admiral nodded and moved off with his aide trailing.

Commander Nuevos walked up beside Jen. "Looks like you might get a medal out of this, Jen. You deserve one."

"I don't need a medal," Jen whispered, watching the admiral leave. "I've got what I've wanted."

Somebody in authority had finally said they were sorry.

Almost exactly six weeks later, Jen stood uncomfortably in ranks as medals and commendations were handed out. When her name was called, Jen marched smartly forward, standing at attention as Captain Dila read a long citation, her mind only catching parts of the recitation. "For meritorious service in military operations against irregular forces on 6 July, 2104 . . . extremely rapid and effective response . . . outstanding initiative . . . coolness and courage against an aggressive and determined enemy . . . in keeping with the highest traditions of military service . . ."

Admiral Yesenski stepped up, pinning a bronze star medal on Jen, then saluted her.

She saluted back, wishing that Paul could be here.

Afterwards, as the ranks dissolved and everyone mingled, Jen's data pad chirped to announce an incoming message. *Bravo Zulu, Lieutenant.* She didn't need to check the ID to know the Navy's version of "well done" came from her father, currently serving in the Pentagon.

Even if Paul was sitting waiting to see the ceremony, it would take at least half an hour for the video to reach Mars and any message to come back. Sighing, Jen pocketed her data pad again.

A moment later a female chief master-at-arms sidled up to Jen. "Lieutenant Shen? Chief Sharpe has mentioned you a few times. Do you remember him?"

"Ivan Sharpe? Yes, of course. I knew him when we were both on the *Michaelson*, and Sharpe worked directly for my husband for a couple of years." As the sole law enforcement professional on the *Michaelson*, Sharpe had been nicknamed "Sheriff," a title he took some pride in.

The master-at-arms nodded, looking nervous. "Lieutenant Sinclair? That's who I really need. Ma'am, Sharpe's in trouble. Could your husband -?"

"My husband is stationed on Mars at the moment."

"Oh." The master-at-arms appeared crestfallen.

"What's the matter? What kind of trouble is Sharpe in? I thought I saw him in ranks earlier."

"He was here, ma'am, but I can't say anything else." The master-at-arms began to back away.

Jen closed the distance. "Can't say? Why not?"

"Ma'am, it's all classified, I can't say anything, I'm sorry I troubled you."

Jen stepped closer. "It's just you and me, chief, and then this conversation never happened."

The chief looked around nervously. "It's classified, ma'am, and nobody told me you have an authorized need to know."

"If Sharpe needs help, I need to know in order to help him. But I heard nothing from you. Not a word. Now what's going on?"

"There's going to be a court-martial," the chief spoke quickly and quietly. "I shouldn't be telling you even that. If anyone finds out I could get busted for it."

"A court-martial? Sharpe is facing a court-martial?" That sounded too ridiculous to be true. Aside from being a wise-ass on occasion, Sharpe had been a model master-at-arms. "Why? And why is it being kept secret?"

The chief grimaced. "Security. Stuff about the attack on the station and vulnerabilities. That's all I know. The charges are secret. Sharpe knows them but can't tell me or anyone else. I can't even find out the names of the officers and chiefs assigned to the court-martial."

"You mean the counsels? The prosecution and defense?"

"No, ma'am. I got the defense counsel's name out of Sharpe. I mean the, what do you call them –"

"Members?" Jen asked with a tightening in her gut.

"Yes, ma'am, members."

A classified court-martial. Even the charges kept secret. "Chief, the only courts-martial that have members are general courts-martial." The most serious kind.

"I know, ma'am." The chief looked around again. "Sharpe thinks he can convince the members that whatever he's charged with isn't true."

Jen let out a half-scornful/half-pained laugh. "Being innocent doesn't always work. Will Sharpe talk to me?"

"No, ma'am. I asked. He says you've seen enough trouble and violating orders by talking to you would just get both him and you in more trouble."

"Thanks for letting me know." Jen looked down at the new medal on her breast, thinking of how her re-won professional status might vanish again if she took the wrong steps now. But that just made her mad, and she knew exactly what Paul would do if he were here. "What's the name of that defense counsel?"

Lieutenant Turen didn't seem thrilled to see Jen. "I can't discuss it. I'm sorry."

"Since when are courts-martial classified?" Jen demanded.

"National security. I can't say any more."

Jen took a deep breath and spoke calmly. "I want to help."

"Lieutenant Shen, I'll give Chief Master-at-Arms Sharpe the best defense possible."

"Defense against what?"

"I can't discuss the charges."

Feeling her jaw tighten, Jen stepped back. The best defense possible? Turen couldn't provide that. She knew who could. She also hated the idea of dialing that number and talking to that person. *It's*

not about you, Jen. It's about Sharpe, and Paul. They never let you down.
"Fine. Excuse me."

Do you really think I can be blown off that easily, Lieutenant Turen?

Jen waited, fighting off a constant urge to shut down the call request. Punching in the number had actually been harder than forcing herself to crawl into the wreckage of the *Maury*, harder than dealing with the attack on the station.

The alert finally beeped and the screen blinked once before steadying into the image of a female commander sitting at her desk. Partially visible behind her was a window opening on a blue sky flecked with clouds. Earth. An open window. Blue sky. The longer Jen was out here the more alien her home world seemed.

"Yes?" the commander asked, conveying the impression of someone interrupted in the middle of important tasks. Then she focused on Jen and jerked with surprise before her expression settled into controlled wariness. "Lieutenant Shen. This is a surprise."

"Commander Carr." Jen swallowed, now trying to overcome an urge to speak angrily. "I . . . I . . ." The words wouldn't come, sticking in her throat.

Carr leaned forward slightly, wariness mixing with concern now. "Is something wrong, lieutenant?"

"Not with me. Not this time." Jen almost winced as those sentences shot free. "I'm . . . sorry, commander. I didn't mean –"

Even with the time-lag between Earth and Franklin Station, Carr had time to interrupt Jen. "You don't owe me any apologies, lieutenant. What's the matter? Legal trouble?"

"A friend of mine." The words finally came in a rush. "A friend of Paul's. Chief Master-at-Arms Ivan Sharpe."

"Sharpe?" Carr frowned in thought. "He helped us get Lieutenant Silver, and Lieutenant Pullman."

"Yes, ma'am. There's a court-martial. A classified court-martial." Jen spilled what little she knew, speaking as if briefing a superior officer, while Carr listened intently. "I was hoping you could tell me how to help Chief Sharpe."

"You think I can help?" Carr settled back, eyeing Jen.

"Yes. Paul made me download your contact info because he said you told him to contact you if he ever needed it. He's not here, he can't help, but I know he'd want to do what he could for Sharpe. Paul always said you were a very good lawyer, and . . . and you always did what . . . what you thought was right."

"As opposed to doing what really was right?" Carr closed her eyes for a moment, before sighing and focusing back on Jen. "I'm still haunted by the thought that I might have won your conviction, lieutenant. I don't know if that brings you any comfort. Let me look into this. I can't give any decent advice without knowing more. How long do we have?"

"I don't know, ma'am. Every time I try to find out anything I'm told it's classified and I have no need to know."

Carr stared at Jen. "That's one hell of a way to run a legal proceeding, lieutenant. It sounds like they're trying to keep this as quiet as possible. What kind of court-martial is it? Could you find that out?"

"Yes, ma'am. It's a general."

Commander Carr's stare intensified. "Give me a contact address for you, lieutenant. I'll call you back. Soon."

"Thank you, ma'am."

But Carr had already broken the connection. Jen glared at the blank screen, wondering if she had debased herself by asking for help from Carr for nothing.

Two days later her data pad chirped urgently. Jen blinked herself awake, wondering what in engineering had broken this time. Either that or someone had fallen sick and needed someone else to stand their watch.

But when she answered the call, Jen saw Commander Carr. The lawyer seemed to be somewhere crowded and her image was slightly tilted, so she was making her call using her own data pad. "Lieutenant Shen?"

"Yes, ma'am."

"Listen, we're not going to have much time. You and I need to hit the deck running on this. Can you get any leave from your current job?"

"Ma'am?" Jen nodded. "Leave? Sure."

"Good. I want you to meet me the day after tomorrow at 0800. That's when my shuttle is supposed to be off-loading. It's cutting it close since the court-martial is supposed to start at 1000 that morning, but it's the best I can do."

Jen stared at the screen. "You're coming up here?"

Carr nodded, her eyes on Jen's. "I owe you, lieutenant. Even if I didn't owe Paul for his assistance in the past, I owe you for the role I played in what almost happened to you and the effect of that on your career since. I had to pass off the cases I was working on to other lawyers in my office and get a priority shuttle lift arranged, but I'll do everything I can for Chief Sharpe. I assume you won't object to me acting as his military attorney."

"No." Jen kept staring stupidly at the screen.

"Good. Don't tell anyone I'm coming up there. I've coordinated already with the defense counsel, but we want to surprise the trial counsel." Carr grinned fiercely in a way that Jen remembered from the courts-martial of Silver and Pullman.

To her own surprise, Jen felt herself smiling back. "I honestly did not expect this, ma'am."

"It'll take a lot more than this to balance the scales, lieutenant," Carr assured her. "Besides, classified trials offend my sense of fair play. I've never approved of the idea." She paused. "Stay away from Sharpe until I get up there. I need you untainted by claims of improper contact."

"Why?" Jen asked, suspicions arising again despite her best intentions.

"Didn't I tell you? You'll be my assistant. That's the only way to get you into that courtroom, and I want you in that courtroom."

The familiar shape of Commander Carr came striding briskly through the crowd. Jen waved to catch her attention, then waited as Carr came up. "All right, lieutenant. Do you have the time off you need?"

"Yes, ma'am."

"Good." Carr started walking again and Jen followed. "The government really wants to keep a lid on this and is insisting that in order to protect classified information only people with legitimate roles in the trial will be allowed to attend. I hope you can live with being my gofer for a while."

Jen nodded. "As long as you don't expect me to get coffee for you."

"No. I don't drink the stuff," Carr confessed. "Herbal tea is my speed."

"Ugh." Jen shuddered. "I need my caffeine, ma'am."

Carr checked the time and exhaled heavily. "I could probably use some of that myself today. I wish they'd served breakfast on that shuttle."

Jen pulled out a breakfast bar. "I thought you might need this. I can't do anything about the tea, though."

"You're forgiven. Thanks." Carr looked around, then focused back on Jen as they moved onto one of the station's main thoroughfares. "Okay. By all appearances no one really planned for this to turn into a general court-martial. Someone insisted on pressing charges, they seemed plausible, and by the time anyone realized the seriousness of the charges would mandate a general court-martial instead of just a summary or a special the ball had rolled far enough downhill and gained enough momentum that no one could stop it. Now the government wants to do it quick, wants to do it clean, and wants to keep it under the radar."

"Why?" Jen asked.

"Because it deals with too many sensitive security issues, and it's happening at a time when the government still wants to be publicly focusing on the heroes who defended Franklin, instead of one of those defenders it alleges criminally failed in his duty." She held out a warding hand before Jen could speak. "I can't lay out the charges for you, yet. You'll hear them at the trial. I've been talking to Turen and he's got a decent foundation of material and witnesses together. But I want you backstopping me because you're a very good engineer."

"Oh, is that a good thing, now?" Jen asked.

Carr grimaced. "Yes."

Jen realized that she'd just twisted a knife, and to her own surprise felt contrite about it. "Sorry," she muttered almost too low for Carr to hear.

"I used that against you once. I deserved the dig." Carr halted suddenly and turned to face Jen. "I had a choice on whether or not to take this case. I promise you I'll do my best to win it. Major Hue, the trial counsel, is a very good and very experienced lawyer. Lieutenant Turen is well intentioned but inexperienced. Hue would have had him for dinner."

"I guess the government wants to win this case," Jen said.

"The government wants to win every case," Carr corrected. "But we work under a system that forces the government to give defendants a fighting chance, when that system is allowed to work. You have precious little reason to believe that, I know, but it's true."

Jen let a pained smile show. "I believe you, commander. After all, when it turned out the government had broken the rules my own case was thrown out by the judge."

"Exactly. Mind you, I don't think anything like that is happening this time. The case seems based on Sharpe's actions and different interpretations of what he did do and should have done, and the consequences of all that."

"I didn't go near Sharpe, but I talked to the master-at-arms who first tipped me off to the court-martial. Master Chief Wilmont, who initiated the charges, doesn't like Sharpe," Jen said. "Hasn't liked him since well before the attack on the station."

"Is that so?" Carr made some quick notes on her data pad. "Do you know why?"

"Yes, ma'am. A bar fight."

"A bar fight? Sharpe?"

"Yes, ma'am. Master Chief Wilmont had a few, claimed I got away with murder and he and Sharpe ending up punching each other out. The senior enlisted community covered up the whole thing, but Wilmont didn't forget." Jen shrugged. "More fall-out from my court-martial." More collateral damage to those who knew her.

Carr looked steadily at Jen for a moment, then a grim smile appeared on her face. "We may use that, lieutenant, and maybe educate Master Chief Wilmont a little in the process. Thanks. What's the name of the enlisted who told you about this?"

"Henga. Chief Master-at-Arms Jan Henga."

"Are she and Sharpe involved?"

"Not as far as I can tell. I think she'd like that but it hasn't happened so far."

"Good. Now, you get to the courtroom. You'll be listed as Lieutenant Turen's assistant on the access list. Sit behind the defense desk and wait."

"You're not coming now?"

"No." Carr smiled reassuringly. "I have a few tasks to do first. Don't worry, I'll be there."

Fifteen minutes later Jen arrived at the courtroom and found an unusual level of security. The panel beside the main entry which was supposed to display case information instead declared "Proceedings closed by order of Commander, U.S. Space Forces." Outside the entry three masters-at-arms stood, turning aside the curious. Jen felt a quiver inside as memories of her pre-trial confinement came back, memories of a hundred small indignities inflicted by cops like these who had been certain she was guilty. Setting her jaw and squaring her shoulders, Jen walked steadily up to the masters-at-arms. "Lieutenant Shen. I'm authorized entry."

One of the masters-at-arms stared at her. Jen remembered the face, and just stared back until the woman averted her eyes. Another master-at-arms was busy checking her ID against his list. "Assistant to the counsel for the defense?" He seemed puzzled. "A line officer, ma'am?"

"I have some experience with legal matters," Jen replied. "Is there a problem?"

"No, ma'am, except you're required to sign this security agreement prior to entry."

Jen read through the document, a standard nondisclosure agreement, then signed. "Anything else?"

"No, ma'am. Thank you, ma'am." The master-at-arms held open the door to the courtroom and Jen walked inside.

Despite all of her mental preparations, the feelings almost overwhelmed her. The despair, the humiliation, the confusion as the government had steadily piled up circumstantial evidence claiming she had sabotaged her own ship. It took all of Jen's self-control to shake off the feeling of panic that rose within her. *I wish Paul was here.*

She knew where the defendant's table was, and paused for a moment looking at it in front of her before taking a seat in the first row of chairs behind the table. Aside from the lack of spectators, the courtroom had a standard arrangement, with the judge's elevated bench in front, the witness chair beside it, the defense and trial counsels' desks facing the judge's bench, rows of empty chairs normally for the use of spectators behind them, and off to one side a long table draped with a Navy blue cloth where the members of the court would sit. She wondered who those members, the jury in this court-martial, would be.

Lieutenant Turen arrived soon afterwards, giving Jen a worried look but nodding in greeting. Some time later the trial counsel arrived. Major Hue seemed quietly competent, his Marine uniform a contrast to the Navy uniforms of the others. At one point Major Hue spotted Jen, frowned, and consulted his data pad. He gave Jen a curious look, but then went back to his preparations.

Half an hour before the trial was scheduled to begin Chief Sharpe came striding down the aisle between the spectator chairs and straight to the defense table. Sharpe, in his finest uniform, greeted Lieutenant Turen, then as he was sitting down noticed Jen, initial surprise turning into a worried glower. "Ma'am, what the –"

Jen silenced him with a look. "At ease, Sheriff. I'm helping the defense."

Sharpe looked toward Turen. "But –"

"I already know. Stay focused, chief."

Just before 1000 the bailiff walked through the courtroom looking for problems, then back to stand by the door through which the judge would enter. "All rise."

Everyone came to attention, and Captain Halstead walked up to the judge's bench, taking his seat. "This Article 39(A) session is called to order. You may be seated."

Major Hue stood. "The court-martial is convened by general court-martial convening order 0334, Commander, United States Space Forces, copies of which have been furnished to the military judge, counsel, and the accused. The charges have been properly referred to the court-martial for trial and were served on the accused on 18 August 2104. The accused and the following persons detailed to the court-martial are present: Captain Halstead, Major Hue, Lieutenant Commander Nasser, Lieutenant Brook, Captain Daldaros, Lieutenant Turen, Master Chief Petty Officer Kobo, Senior Chief Petty Officer Polaski."

"Very well. Bailiff, please ask the members of the court-martial to enter."

The bailiff went to another door, cracked it, nodded, then stood aside. "All rise."

Jen watched as the members entered. LCDR Nasser was a space warfare officer. He'd likely be tough. Lieutenant Brook was an intelligence officer, so it was hard to tell what she'd be like. Captain Daladros, a Marine whose rank was equivalent to a Navy lieutenant's, bore an impressive set of ribbons on the left breast of her uniform. Master Chief Kobo was a radio specialist, while Senior Chief Polaski was a bosun's mate.

"You may be seated," the judge ordered the rest of the courtroom again as soon as the members had sat down. "Continue, Trial Counsel."

First Major Hue and then Lieutenant Turen faced the judge's bench, each reciting the standard legal boilerplate establishing that they had been properly assigned to the court-martial, were qualified and sworn, and had not acted in any way that might disqualify them from serving in the court-martial.

Captain Halstead looked at Sharpe. "Chief Petty Officer Ivan Sharpe, you have the right to be represented in this court-martial by Lieutenant Turen, your detailed defense counsel, or you may be represented by military counsel of your selection, if the counsel you request is reasonably available. If you are represented by military counsel of your own selection, you would lose the right to have Lieutenant Turen, your detailed counsel, continue to help in your defense. Do you understand?"

Sharpe, standing also, spoke clearly. "Yes, sir. I understand."

"In addition, you have the right to be represented by civilian counsel, at no expense to the United States. Civilian counsel may represent you alone or along with your military counsel. Do you understand?"

"Yes, sir."

"Do you have any questions about your right to counsel?"

"No, sir."

"Who do you want to represent you?"

"Your Honor, I wish to be represented by a military attorney of my choice. Commander Alexandra Carr, United States Navy."

The courtroom went totally silent, the judge and trial counsel staring at Sharpe and the few other occupants watching them. Finally, Captain Halstead cleared his throat. "You understand, Chief Sharpe, that you are allowed to request a specific military attorney but that the attorney must be reasonably available?"

"I do, Your Honor."

Major Hue shook his head. "Your Honor, Trial Counsel wishes to point out that Commander Carr is currently stationed on Earth." He held up his data pad. "I have just confirmed that she is assigned to the Joint Legal Team for the Washington Military District. While not wishing to deny Chief Petty Officer Sharpe his right to chose his own counsel for the defense, I must argue that this does not meet any accepted definition of 'reasonably available.'"

Lieutenant Turen stood up, his expression apologetic. "Your Honor, notwithstanding Commander Carr's assigned duty station, it is my understanding that Commander Carr is currently physically located just outside of this courtroom."

This time the silence reigned longer. Finally, Judge Halstead pointed toward the door. "Why don't we ask her to join us, Defense Counsel?" Lieutenant Turen walked quickly to the back of the courtroom, opened the door, then stood aside as Commander Carr walked in.

Jen barely kept from laughing at the expression on Major Hue's face. The judge couldn't seem to decide whether to smile or to frown, but finally settled on a scowl. "I don't approve of theatrics in my courtroom. Who were trying to impress with that little show, Commander Carr?"

Carr stopped before the judge's bench, speaking respectfully. "My apologies if this appeared theatrical, Your Honor. The government's insistence on limiting access to the courtroom forced me to remain outside until I was named by the defendant as his choice for counsel."

Halstead didn't appear to be mollified by the explanation. "How long have you been on this station, commander?"

"I arrived on this morning's shuttle, Your Honor."

"You've been on the station less than two hours? Do you feel capable of acting as counsel for the defense, or will that require the court to order a recess to give you time to prepare?"

"I've been in contact with Lieutenant Turen and feel capable of acting as Chief Petty Officer Sharpe's counsel in this trial without need for a recess, Your Honor."

The judge studied Carr for a while, his eyes intent, then nodded. "Trial Counsel, does the government have any cause for challenge against Commander Carr?"

Major Hue gave Carr a hard look. "Given the classified nature of these proceedings, the government feels it is necessary to establish what brought Commander Carr to this station at this time and led her to be in contact with Lieutenant Turen, Your Honor."

Carr nodded, perfectly calm and composed. "I initiated contact with Lieutenant Turen when informal information from other sources revealed that Chief Sharpe was facing trial, Your Honor. Those sources notified me only of the fact of a trial, not of specific charges, evidence or other classified information. I received formal approval from my chain of command to discuss the case with Lieutenant Turen prior to contacting him."

"Why did you get involved?" the judge asked. "Are you saying you are personally acquainted with Chief Sharpe, commander?"

Carr turned slightly to indicate Sharpe. "I know him because he was a witness in some of the cases I prosecuted while assigned here, Your Honor. He rendered important assistance to my cases."

"That scarcely seems adequate reason to become so involved in this case, commander," the judge pressed.

"I had other personal reasons for visiting the station and getting involved in the case, Your Honor, which I will be happy to discuss with the judge and Trial Counsel in closed session."

"Personal reasons?" Halstead asked. His eyes came to rest on Jen before going back to Carr. "The court is willing to accept Commander Carr's explanation. Does Trial Counsel wish to insist upon a formal challenge to her presence here?"

Hue seemed to be thinking, and now shook his head. "No, Your Honor."

Halstead waved toward the defendant's table. "Then you may assume your duties as counsel for the defense, commander. Lieutenant Turen, you are excused."

Lieutenant Turen spoke with a trace of pleading in his voice. "Your Honor, I respectfully request that the court allow me to remain as an observer for the trial."

"Does the government object?" the judge asked.

Major Hue smiled crookedly. "Lieutenant Turen is already fully aware of all matters in this case, Your Honor, and observing the trial would no doubt provide him with invaluable experience. He can serve as Defense Counsel's assistant."

Carr smiled politely. "Defense Counsel has no objection to Lieutenant Turen observing the trial, but desires to retain her current assistant."

Hue shook his head. "Your Honor, I didn't intend making an issue of Lieutenant Shen's presence in this courtroom, but in conjunction with Commander Carr, I believe her presence might be prejudicial to a fair and impartial trial."

"Is Trial Counsel suggesting that the current case bears any relationship to the case involving Lieutenant Shen?" Carr asked.

"Of course not. But the members might erroneously draw such a connection."

Carr was in full lawyer mode, addressing the judge with precise and earnest words. "Your Honor, the charges against Lieutenant Shen were dismissed with prejudice. As far as the government is concerned, nothing regarding those charges or her court-martial prior to that dismissal can ever be used against Lieutenant Shen. If she is excluded from this courtroom on the grounds that she was so charged, then the government will be taking prejudicial actions against Lieutenant Shen solely on the basis of those charges and that trial. Such a challenge cannot be legally admissible."

Halstead was listening, his mouth twisted, one hand slowly turning the gavel he held. "Defense Counsel makes an excellent point, Trial Counsel. Do you have a rebuttal?"

Major Hue looked down for a long moment, then raised his eyes and shook his head. "No, Your Honor. Trial Counsel will raise no further objection to the assistant for the Defense Counsel."

"Very well." Halstead looked at Carr, his face stern again. "But if any more theatrics take place, including any involving your assistant, commander, then I will revisit this issue. Is that understood?"

"Yes, Your Honor. I now request five minutes to assume duties as defense counsel."

"Granted." Halstead waved one hand in permission and Carr walked over to the defense table, unsmiling. "Thanks," she told Turen as he vacated his seat, then Carr turned toward Sharpe. "How are you feeling, Chief?"

Sharpe seemed to be trying not to grin as he looked from Carr to Jen. "Better than I have in quite a while, ma'am."

"Good, but even Lieutenant Shen and I can't guarantee the outcome of this trial. Look professional, look concerned, look offended if appropriate. Don't look cocky or confident. Understand?"

"Yes, ma'am."

Three minutes later Major Hue walked to stand before the judge's bench. "The general nature of the charges in this case allege failure to follow lawful orders in the face of the enemy, which actions in turn placed at additional hazard a major government installation. The charges were preferred by Commander, United States Naval Space Forces, and forwarded with recommendations as to disposition to Commander, United States Space Forces. Your Honor, are you aware of any matter which may be a ground for challenge against you?"

"I am aware of none," Halstead replied.

"The government has no challenge for cause against the military judge."

Commander Carr stood. "The defense has no challenge for cause against the military judge."

Halstead faced Sharpe again. "Chief Sharpe, do you understand that you have the right to be tried by a court-martial composed of members and that, if you are found guilty of any offense, those members would determine a sentence?"

"Yes, sir."

"Do you also understand that you may request in writing or orally here in the court-martial trial before me alone, and that if I approve such a request, there will be no members and I alone will decide whether you are guilty and, if I find you guilty, determine a sentence?"

"Yes, sir."

"Have you discussed these choices with your counsel?"

"I have, sir."

"By which type of court-martial do you choose to be tried?"

Sharpe didn't hesitate. "By members, sir."

"Very well. The accused will now be arraigned."

Major Hue faced toward Sharpe as well. "All parties and the military judge have been furnished a copy of the charges and specifications. Does the accused want them read?"

Sharpe, still on his feet, nodded as he replied. "Yes, sir, I do."

"Very well. Chief Master-at-Arms Ivan Sharpe is charged with violations of the following articles of the Uniform Code of Military Justice.

"Article 91, Insubordinate conduct toward warrant officer, noncommissioned officer, or petty officer. In that Chief Petty Officer

Ivan Sharpe, United States Navy, having received a lawful order from Peter Wilmont, a master chief petty officer, then known by the said Ivan Sharpe to be a master chief petty officer, to immediately fire upon an individual who was one of the terrorists then assaulting Franklin Naval Station, an order which it was his duty to obey, did, on board Benjamin Franklin Naval Space Station, on or about 6 July 2104, willfully disobey the same.

"Article 92, Failure to obey order or regulation. In that…Ivan Sharpe…having knowledge of a lawful order issued by Master Chief Petty Officer Peter Wilmont to immediately fire upon an individual who was one of the terrorists then assaulting Franklin Naval Station, an order which it was his duty to obey, did…fail to obey the same.

"Article 99, Misbehavior before the enemy. Specification One. In that…Ivan Sharpe…did…in the presence of the enemy, endanger the safety of Franklin Naval Station, which it was his duty to defend, by disobeying an order from Master Chief Petty Officer Peter Wilmont to engage the enemy. Specification Two. In that… Ivan Sharpe…being in the presence of the enemy, did…by refusing an order to engage the enemy, willfully fail to do his utmost to defeat that enemy, as it was his duty to do.

"Article 108, Military property of the United States – sale, loss, damage, destruction or wrongful disposition. In that…Ivan Sharpe…did…without proper authority, willfully suffer a large section of Franklin Naval Station, military property of the United States, to be damaged by allowing enemy forces additional time to commit acts of destruction against said property.

"The charges are signed by Commander, United States Naval Space Forces, a person subject to the code, as accuser; are properly sworn to before a commissioned officer of the armed forces authorized to administer oaths, and are properly referred to this court-martial for trial by Commander, United States Space Forces, the convening authority."

Jen tried to keep her face calm as the charges were read. She knew some of them had to be serious to justify a general court-martial, but it had still been difficult to hear Sharpe charged with misbehavior before the enemy.

Captain Halstead turned to Sharpe again. "Chief Sharpe, how do you plead? Before receiving your pleas, I advise you that any motions to dismiss any charge or grant other relief should be made at this time."

Commander Carr stood for a moment. "The defense has no motions at this time."

Sharpe, his uniform and bearing so perfect that he looked like a recruiting advertisement for the service, faced the members. "I plead not guilty to all charges and specifications."

"Very well," the judge responded. "Does the prosecution have an opening statement?"

"I do, Your Honor." Major Hue looked toward Sharpe, then at the members. "During the assault upon Franklin Naval Station last July, the very survival of the station and the personnel embarked on the station demanded the utmost from all personnel. In this time of crisis, Chief Petty Officer Sharpe willfully failed to live up to those demands, instead taking actions which resulted in increased risk to this station and everyone upon it. Chief Sharpe should be found guilty as to all charges and specifications, for his failures not only imperiled this station and its personnel, but also acted to negate the sacrifices of those dying to save it."

Commander Carr walked out in front of the defense table as Major Hue sat down. "The defense contends that, contrary to the charges lodged against him, Chief Sharpe did everything possible to defend this station, that his actions were appropriate and proper under the circumstances, and that claims his action increased the peril to Franklin Naval Station are exaggerated and without foundation."

Carr returned to the defense table and the judge indicated Major Hue. "You may proceed, Trial Counsel."

"Thank you, Your Honor. The prosecution calls as its first witness Captain Karl Dila."

Jen's department head walked into the courtroom with the slightly-distracted air he usually wore, as if Dila was constantly mentally calculating stress coefficients in surrounding structures. As he took his seat in the witness chair, Major Hue stood respectfully before him. "Do you swear that the evidence you give in the case now in hearing shall be the truth, the whole truth, and nothing but the truth, so help you God?"

"Yes, I do."

"Are you Captain Karl Dila, United States Navy, assigned to the engineering department on Benjamin Franklin Naval Space Station?"

"Yes. I'm in charge of the engineering department."

Major Hue gestured and a very large schematic of the station appeared on one wall of the courtroom. "Did you participate in the engineering analysis of the actions of those who attacked Franklin Naval Station on 6 July?"

"I did. I led the analysis team. I also ultimately assumed command in engineering central on the day of the attack."

"Trial Counsel asks that the engineering analysis be entered into the court record. Captain, what was your conclusion as to the goal of the attackers?"

Dila paused as if trying to make sure he understood the exact meaning of the question. "Ultimately, they wanted to destroy the station."

Major Hue nodded. "Were the attackers equipped with weapons capable of destroying the station?"

"Not directly," Dila answered with an engineer's precision. "That would have required very large amounts of conventional explosives, which the station's sensors would have surely detected on their approach because of the size and mass involved. Or nuclear weapons, and those would have been spotted by us even earlier due to radiation leakage. No, the attackers intended to create conditions under which the station would destroy itself as a result of free surface effect. They could do that while carrying small enough quantities of explosives to remain undetected on their approach to the station."

"What exactly is free surface effect?" Hue asked.

Dila took on the expression of an engineer explaining to lesser beings how the world works. "In laymen's terms, it's what happens when a liquid is in a partially-filled container. On a ship at sea, as the ship heels to one side the liquid will react by flowing toward the low side, increasing the force of the heel. When the ship swings the other way, the liquid once again rushes to the 'low' side in a delayed reaction which further increases the force destabilizing the ship. The higher up in the structure the liquid is, and the larger the space available to move in, the worse the resulting effect. That's why ships use a number of tanks to hold liquid instead of one big tank, and keep the tanks low in the ship."

"How could this phenomenon effect a space station?"

"Because the water tanks are high up in the disc, toward the center. It allows us to feed water 'downhill' to the rest of the station and provides substantial mass in the lower gravity areas near the station's core. Once the tanks were breeched, the water followed the forces created by the rotation of the disc to simulate gravity. Those forces are both outward and to the side, because of the rotation. But the station is designed to automatically compensate for shifts in mass. As the water rushed to one side and down, it redistributed mass, and the station automatically shifted other mass and altered rotational velocity to compensate."

Dila pointed to the display, where an animation began playing out. "That compensation created forces shifting the water back up and in the other direction. As the water surged up and to the other side, with more force now, the mass distribution control systems tried to compensate again by shifting larger quantities of mass down and over and again altering rotation speed, which caused the free-flowing water to start rolling even more heavily down and in the original direction. Every shift in forces inside the station tended to reinforce the motion of the water, giving it more energy. On a ship, this eventually results in the ship heeling too far over and capsizing. On this station, the forces would have eventually exceeded the ability of the structure to contain them."

Dila paused, thinking. "It's the same sort of thing that happens when you're carrying a pan partially filled with water, and the water seems to start sloshing back and forth with a life of its own until it surges over one side of the pan. Free surface effect and the delayed feedback from your own attempts to compensate."

Major Hue nodded, his face grim. "But in this case the station would have been torn apart."

"A big piece of it, yes, major," Dila agreed. "The remainder of the station would have still been rotating but without the structural integrity. The models we've run produce different results as to how much more of the station would have subsequently come apart, but there wouldn't have been much left by the time any remaining portions could be stabilized."

"Then the attack had a significant possibility of succeeding in destroying Franklin Naval Station?"

"Yes, that was our conclusion, if by destroying you mean more than sixty percent structural loss."

Major Hue nodded again, heavily this time, his expression somber. "How important was it to counter the actions of the attackers as soon as possible, to stop their assault, to reoccupy the damaged areas and begin damage control?"

Captain Dila waved one hand at the schematic. "Absolutely critical. Every second counted. That's one of the reasons we believe the attackers seized engineering central, to prevent us from initiating corrective overrides of the automated stabilization systems. They probably also intended to download software which would have magnified the over-compensation of the stabilization systems and caused other problems for us, but couldn't because all of the consoles had been secured and control functions redistributed. We can't confirm that since all of the attackers' software was destroyed, but it seems very likely."

Major Hue nodded. "'Every . . . second . . . counted.'" He let the quote hang for a moment before speaking again. "You believe then, that in light of the damage the attackers had caused in the time available to them, this station might well have been destroyed if you had not very quickly recognized the danger –"

"Excuse me," Captain Dila interrupted, "but I didn't realize the danger first. That was Lieutenant Shen, over there." Everyone turned to look at Jen, who hastily sat straighter. With an engineer's obliviousness to the reactions of others, including Major Hue, Dila continued on blithely. "That's one of the reasons she got that medal. I didn't know she'd be here, though. You didn't need both of us to testify on engineering matters."

Hue was still trying to come up with words when Commander Carr rose smoothly to her feet. "I'm sorry, Captain Dila, but Lieutenant Shen isn't in this courtroom as a witness in the case. She's volunteered to assist the defense."

"Oh. All right." Dila turned back to Hue, who briefly looked daggers at Carr.

Judge Halstead said nothing, but shook his head at Commander Carr, who feigned innocence.

The members were watching Jen intently. She realized that this had been Carr's plan all along, to bring to the members' attention that one of those recognized for the defense of the station was now working to defend Sharpe. No wonder Major Hue hadn't been able to hide his unhappiness.

"If I may summarize, captain," Major Hue began again, "there was a real possibility that the attackers would succeed in causing this station to tear itself apart, and it was critically important to counter their actions as soon as possible. Is that right?"

Dila paused as if thinking through the statement, then nodded. "Yes."

"Thank you, captain. No more questions."

Commander Carr walked over to stand before Captain Dila. "Sir, when you did the analysis of the attackers' plans, did you discover a major error on their part in the execution of their plan?"

Dila frowned in thought. "You mean the fourth water tank?"

"Yes, sir. The fourth water tank. The attackers blew open three water tanks, is that correct? But instead of blowing open a fourth, they instead set their charges against a bulkhead with no water tank behind it."

"That's right." Dila leaned forward, pointing at the schematic. "You see, they must have been working off of old station plans. A year old at least. In the intervening period, there'd been some internal modifications to increase structural stability, storage capacity and other things. On the old plans, that bulkhead confined the fourth water tank. But the tank's limits were moved a great deal to port, you see here, on the far side and a little to port on the near side. The work was finished about three months before the attack. Of course, the tactic might still have worked. The fourth tank was insurance, to guarantee the station's destruction, but the three they did blow open could have done the job."

Carr shook her head, looking perplexed. "But they didn't. Weren't the bulkheads marked with standard identifying data?"

"Absolutely. The bulkhead the attackers blew open was labeled spares storage and the new one was labeled liquid storage. All according to regulation. But the attackers undoubtedly had orders laid out in their data pads specifying exactly what to do and where, so that's what they did."

Commander Carr seemed skeptical. "The attackers ignored clear identifying signs and instead followed orders exactly?"

"That's right. When we analyzed their actions based on damage and time lines and all the other available evidence it became clear that they moved very quickly and precisely for the first part of their attack, but when something unexpected was encountered they didn't seem to know what to do. Like when they captured engineering central and found all of the consoles shut down. They apparently just waited there afterwards until the Marines came through." Dila waved vaguely. "We consulted with experts on terrorism, and they all concurred that the people sent on suicide attacks like this aren't leaders or even particularly bright. As one of the experts said, they're smart enough to pull a trigger and dumb enough to believe what their leaders tell them about how great it is to die. So these attackers certainly came in with a detailed plan specifying exactly what to do and where to do it. Even though every data pad carried by the attackers was destroyed or wiped we can be certain of that because of our analysis of their actions. They blew that bulkhead there because that's what their orders called for. They may well not even have known *why* they were blowing holes where they did."

"They were just following orders," Carr observed. "Exactly following orders."

"Right. Exactly. That's a good word."

"Sir, some of the charges allege that Chief Sharpe's failure to engage one attacker increased the chances the station would be destroyed. Do you agree with that as an engineer?"

Dila scrunched up his face, one hand rising to rub his neck. "Just one? Where was this? When? I find it hard to believe – Was it when the attackers were first entering the station? At the access trunks?"

Major Hue rose and shook his head. "No, sir. We'll provide a full accounting of that incident to the members lat –"

"If it wasn't then and there I really can't say. Seems odd. Lieutenant Shen? What do you think?"

Jen barely kept from reflexively replying to her commanding officer's question before the judge rapped his gavel on the bench. "I'm sorry, captain," Halstead said, "but Lieutenant Shen hasn't been called as a witness in this case and cannot testify."

"Well, all right," Captain Dila conceded. "But you really ought to ask her, too."

Commander Carr nodded with a serious expression. "Thank you, captain."

Judge Halstead gave a narrow-eyed look at Carr as she returned to her seat, then glanced at Major Hue. "Does Trial Counsel wish to redirect?"

"Briefly, Your Honor." Hue stood up but didn't leave his table. "Captain Dila, notwithstanding the attackers' failure to blow open the fourth water tank, didn't the response to the attack still require the utmost speed? Could any delay have been fatal?"

"Yes. Didn't I already say that? That's why Lieutenant Shen's –"

"Thank you, captain. Were there any uncertainties in your engineering analysis of the threat to the station?"

Dila appeared once again puzzled by the question. "There's always uncertainties, though the scale of them varies."

"Then you can't be one hundred percent certain that one individual's actions couldn't have made a difference one way or the other."

"No. Not one hundred percent," Dila agreed.

"Do the members of the court have questions for the witness?" the judge asked.

LCDR Nasser nodded respectfully to Captain Dila. "Sir, what's the margin of error in your engineering analysis of the results of the attack?"

"Plus or minus one percent," Dila answered instantly.

"Then there's only a one percent chance of significant variation from your results?"

"Yes."

"Including the possibility that one individual's actions could have significantly worsened the results of the attack?"

"Right. Are you an experienced engineer, commander?"

"No, sir," Nasser replied. "I work in Operations."

"You seem to have a good grasp of things despite that," Dila observed.

"The members have no further questions," LCDR Nasser said, one corner of his mouth twitching as he obviously fought down a smile.

Major Hue took a few deep breaths as Dila left the courtroom. "The prosecution calls as its next witness Colonel James Lamont, United States Marine Corps."

Lamont marched to the witness stand as if assaulting an objective, took the oath, then waited, sitting at attention.

Major Hue gestured toward the large projection of Franklin still displayed on one side of the courtroom. "Colonel, did you lead the team analyzing the military aspects of the attack on this station on 6 July?"

"Yes, I did, major."

Hue held up his data pad. "Trial Counsel would like to introduce the military analysis into the court's record. Colonel, could you please explain how the attack on Franklin on 6 July developed?"

"Certainly." Colonel Lamont hunched forward slightly to study the diagram, then nodded and began speaking, using pointers to indicate parts of the image. "The terrorists were launched inside individual stealth pods with just enough power to keep them alive for the duration of their transit. The mass and velocity of individual pods and their shielding were carefully designed to avoid being detected by the station sensors watching for approaching objects. There's no doubt they must have been launched from one of the merchant ships transiting this area well above Franklin Naval Station's orbit, using spring launchers or something similar which provided no signature for us to detect. Whoever planned the attack must have extensively observed and analyzed the station's defenses to identify a path and means of approach which would avoid those defenses."

Lamont indicated an area on top of Franklin's disc, not too far from the hollow core. "They landed in this area between zero one twenty two and zero one twenty four universal solar time. They tried to spoof the locks on the access trunks here and here, but failed because the security protocols had been changed within the last year. The attackers then blew open the access trunks at zero one thirty one, providing the first clear indication of their presence, and entered the station. They subsequently resealed the breaches in the access trunks to keep the water they freed from its tanks from being sucked out into space."

The three-dimensional schematic of Franklin's interior pivoted. "During the next several minutes the attackers fired EMP bursts down passageways they used or passed, burning out sensors, lines and junctions. Within a couple of minutes the station was effectively blind to events in a spreading area while the duty watch standers tried to determine what was going on. The station's emergency response teams were called out at zero one thirty eight as mandated by standing orders in the event of possible external or internal threat activity, but were being deployed without any idea of the nature of the threat. Fortunately, at zero one forty two, Franklin's command structure received the first clear confirmation that an attack was underway, as well as descriptions of the attackers."

Lamont paused, his eyes going to Jen, and he nodded approvingly to her before returning to the diagram. "The attackers had occupied this entire area before the Marines on the USS *Belleau Wood* were called out for combat employment at zero one forty four." Red blotches appeared in scores of places on the schematic. "Explosives brought by the attackers blew open tanks, bulkheads and partitions in many places while the station emergency response teams contained the threat and the Marines deployed for their counterattack."

"Marine counterattacks went in here, here, here and here beginning at zero two one five. Resistance was fanatical, with all but two of the attackers fighting to the death, the two survivors being too badly wounded to suicide. By zero three zero two, all resistance had ceased. Subsequent sweeps confirmed that all attackers had been neutralized. None of their equipment or persons contained any identifying data, and analysis of their equipment indicates a mix of raw materials and components whose geographic origin could not be established. Neither of the two survivors appears to know where they were trained or anything about the ship which launched them." Lamont leaned back, waiting for further questions.

Major Hue indicated the schematic. "Was victory certain, colonel?"

"Victory is never certain, major."

"Our defending forces suffered casualties."

"Correct. Four masters-at-arms dead, several others wounded, and nine Marines wounded."

"Could we have lessened the number of casualties if we'd waited a little longer before counterattacking?" Major Hue asked.

"Probably. But we didn't have the luxury of time."

Hue nodded, his face grim. "Colonel, if you give an order, do you expect it to be obeyed?"

"Of course I do," Lamont replied.

"Do you regard an order given in combat to be any different?"

"Different?" Lamont studied Major Hue. "No. An order is an order. If anything, combat increases the need to know that your orders will be obeyed promptly and correctly."

Major nodded again. "No further questions."

Commander Carr approached the Marine colonel respectfully. "Colonel Lamont, you reported that between zero one thirty three and zero one fifty nine the attackers were blowing open tanks, bulkheads and partitions in the areas they controlled."

"That's correct."

"In other words, the attackers began their demolition activity before the station emergency response teams had even been called out, and continued it until a short time before the Marine counterattack went in."

"That's also correct, commander."

Carr paused, looking at the schematic. "Did the attackers try to break through the defensive perimeter established by the emergency response teams?"

The Marine shook his head. "No. As best we can tell they stopped trying to take new areas by zero two hundred at the latest."

"By zero two hundred at the latest the attackers had gained control of as much of the station as they desired?" Carr asked.

"Objection!" Major Hue pointed at Carr. "Defense Counsel is asking the witness to speculate on matters about which he can have no certain knowledge."

"Objection sustained," Halstead replied immediately. "Counsel for the defense is to ensure her questions are framed appropriately."

"Yes, Your Honor." Carr, seeming unabashed, focused on Lamont again. "Colonel, did the attackers give any indication after zero two hundred that they desired to gain control of more of the station?"

This time Lamont shook his head decisively. "No, commander."

"Was there any indication that the attackers planned to survive the action?"

Lamont snorted. "No. As the report indicates, those who could suicided rather than be captured."

"Then they didn't cease offensive action out of fear of dying in the attempt to seize more of the station? Before zero two hundred they had already done what they needed to do?"

"Objection!" Major Hue gestured toward Carr. "Defense Counsel is once again asking the witness to speculate, this time as to the mindset of dead men and women."

"Your Honor," Carr stated, "I believe the question is firmly grounded in established facts, that the attackers had ceased offensive action and that they did not act in fear of dying during the attack. Surely a Marine colonel is capable of drawing expert conclusions from those facts."

"No one can know why the attackers chose to do or not to do any action or actions," Hue insisted. "None of them can testify to their motives."

"Their established actions testify for them," Carr argued.

Halstead rapped his bench lightly with his gavel. "Both counsels make good points. But Defense Counsel has already established the point she wished to make. Objection sustained. Let's move on, Defense Counsel."

"Yes, Your Honor." Carr faced Lamont again. "Colonel, you reviewed all of the records of the fighting on this station on 6 July? What shape were those records in?"

"While the Marine records were fully intact, the records of the station and its personnel often suffered from gaps and interruptions caused by the damage to the station's sensors and various forms of interference."

Carr nodded. "Have you personally been in combat, Colonel Lamont?"

Lamont smiled very briefly, indicating his ribbons. "A few times, commander."

Walking over to the schematic, Carr indicated the symbols representing station defenders. "Colonel, to what extent did you evaluate the actions of individual defenders? How well or appropriately each responded to whatever they encountered?"

Major Hue was on his feet. "Objection. Your Honor, Defense Counsel is introducing material into cross-examination which was not brought out during the witness's testimony."

Commander Carr spread her hands. "Your Honor, Trial Counsel is the one who introduced the study into this proceeding."

"Your Honor," Hue insisted, "Defense Counsel's question is not germane to the testimony elicited from the witness."

Halstead held up one hand, his expression sour. "Trial Counsel, you introduced the colonel's study into evidence as an exhibit in this trial while questioning the witness. By doing so, you opened up all material in that study to cross-examination. Objection over-ruled. Continue, Defense Counsel."

"Thank you, Your Honor." Carr indicated Colonel Lamont. "Sir? Should I repeat the question?"

"I recall the question." Lamont studied the schematic for a moment. "Of course we evaluated the actions of individuals, not with an eye to punishment or reward because that wasn't our job, but in order to derive whatever lessons we could from the engagement."

Carr gave him a somber look. "How many times when evaluating those actions did you, as a combat veteran, conclude that an individual's actions were clearly wrong?"

Major Hue's face reddened, but he glanced at Halstead, saw the judge's expression, and sat silent.

Lamont spent several moments thinking, then shook his head. "There were any number of cases where we suggested alternatives, things which could have been done differently."

"Differently? Not wrong?"

"That's right." The colonel shifted slightly in his seat, a shadow of memories crossing his face. "Commander, it's one thing to review records after an engagement. It's another thing to be in the middle of that engagement. I can have a perfect picture of whatever had happened but that's not the same as being there when the bullets were flying, the situation was unclear and the pressure was on. Some things can be identified as clearly wrong. Running from the enemy, failing to exercise command, that sort of thing. But most of what we see reflects the uncertainties of the situation as it unfolded. We weren't there, so playing God isn't really appropriate or useful except inasmuch as it identifies problem areas to address in planning, equipment and training."

Carr waited a moment before speaking again. "You weren't there."

"Precisely, commander."

"Did you identify any points where the actions or inactions of a single individual had or could have had a critical effect on the outcome of the events of 6 July?"

Hue was rising to his feet. "Objection. Defense Counsel is leading the witness."

Judge Halstead shook his head. "This clearly falls under the conclusions of the study as well, Trial Counsel. Overruled. The witness may answer the question."

Colonel Lamont gave Hue a slightly bemused look, then focused back on Carr. "In a few cases, yes." He pointed to Jen. "Her actions, for example. If any one person's actions saved the station, it was Lieutenant Shen's." Major Hue had one hand on his forehead, his face lowered, as Jen once again was singled out. "But even in Lieutenant Shen's statement, she properly acknowledged that without the quick actions and support of the watch standers in engineering and the Marines she could not have accomplished what she did."

Carr seemed intrigued by the answer. "Are you saying, Colonel, that even the actions of those whose outstanding performance has been acknowledged would not have made a difference without the support of others?"

"Of course." Lamont spoke firmly, as if lecturing now. "Popular fiction tends to celebrate the solitary hero, the lone wolf, but the real and consistent key to success in action is invariably the team. A group functioning in a coordinated and supporting manner. That's what our training emphasizes, and I know the Navy recognizes the same truth."

"That's in terms of success," Carr noted. "Are you saying the same is true in terms of failure? That you did not identify any individual whose failures stood out as significant?"

"We did not," Colonel Lamont replied. "That doesn't mean it can't happen. A sentry asleep or inattentive could have disastrous results, for example, but our post-engagement analysis did not identify any such case here."

"No such case?" Commander Carr nodded slowly, drawing out the moment. "Thank you, Colonel. No further questions."

"Does Trial Counsel wish to redirect?" Halstead asked.

"Yes, Your Honor." Major Hue indicated the schematic. "Colonel Lamont, when Marines are in combat they are linked to their commanders by a sophisticated command and control system which allows the commanders to see what the individual Marines are seeing and experience what those Marines are experiencing, isn't that correct?"

"No." Lamont shook his head while Hue tried not to frown. "See what they see, yes. Experience what they're experiencing? No. It's the difference between actually being in combat and playing a simulator or video game. The latter might get your adrenaline up, but it's not the same as the former."

"But," Major Hue tried to rally, "don't you routinely give orders to those Marines in combat based upon that information? Tell them exactly what to do?"

Lamont frowned, pondering the question. "Yes and no, major. 'Head that way,' 'engage these forces,' yes, that kind of thing. But exactly? 'Stand here'? 'Move two steps right'? Only under very exceptional circumstances. That's the kind of micromanagement that gets Marines killed."

"But you would order a Marine to engage a particular target and expect that order to be carried out, wouldn't you, sir?"

"Yes. As a rule."

As Major Hue took his seat again, LCDR Nasser addressed the colonel. "Sir, you used the term micromanagement. All of us here, I think, recognize that when we experience it. But you also indicated a command to engage a specific target would not be micromanagement in your view?"

"That really depends," Lamont replied. "In general no, as I said, but there's so many possible circumstances."

"Are there conditions under which you would regard an order to shoot at a specific individual as micromanagement?"

"It *depends*. I'm not there on-scene. I do not routinely pick targets for Marines under my command in combat situations. But if I tell them to engage one, they'd better have a very good reason for not doing so."

Master Chief Kobo frowned. "Sir, how much initiative do you expect your personnel to use in such a situation?"

"As much as they need to," Lamont replied dryly. "I expect them to follow orders but also to use their heads. If I wanted robots who did exactly what they were told and only that then we'd have robots on the frontlines. But that's never worked too well in practice."

Senior Chief Polaski had been looking troubled, and now spoke. "Colonel, you stated that for the most part the actions of individuals didn't make much difference. Is that right? Are you saying the individual actions of the masters-at-arms didn't really matter?"

Lamont shook his head. "No. That's not what I intended to say. Individual actions do matter. The actions of the Navy masters-at-arms were courageous and resolute, and certainly played a very important role in the engagement. But while those Navy personnel displayed individual courage and resolution, it was their work as a team which made the difference. Any single individual trying to stop the attackers, or any group acting as individuals instead of a team, would have failed. A very important part of the accomplishments of the masters-at-arms was that they fought as a team to achieve their objective. Their actions impressed the Marines who fought in the engagement, and that's not easy to do."

Polaski smiled. "Thank you, colonel. I'm very glad to hear that."

The next witness was Master Chief Petty Officer Peter Wilmont. Tall and trim, Wilmont took his seat and avoided looking toward Sharpe.

"Master Chief," Hue began, "could you summarize the events on 6 July which led you to initiate the charges against Chief Sharpe?"

"Certainly, major. The emergency response teams had been called out. The situation remained fluid, but we could identify the areas occupied by the enemy by seeing where sensors had been destroyed. We were ordered to establish a defensive perimeter around that area. I assisted in ordering sections of personnel into position, monitoring their actions and progress and issuing further orders as appropriate."

Wilmont paused for a moment, chewing his lip. "At about zero one fifty I was monitoring the picture from Chief Sharpe's suit when I clearly saw one of the attackers open a hatch and pause in the entry. I ordered Sharpe to fire. Sharpe didn't act. I ordered him to fire again. Sharpe acknowledged the order but did not fire. As I was ordering Sharpe to fire again, he began to argue, then I saw the attacker jerk back through the hatch and close it." The master chief paused again, his face reddening. "Sharpe could have taken out that target. We could have gained control of that hatch much quicker than we did. One more dead attacker, one less position to fight through. It wasn't long after that we heard that the bodies of Chief Yasmin and Petty Officer Hastings had been found not far from that location. They'd been killed, while we couldn't get through that hatch, by an attacker who was still alive."

The courtroom sat silent for a moment after Wilmont finished speaking, then Major Hue walked toward a large display screen. "I will now play back the recording made by station systems of the perspective from Chief Sharpe's suit during the incident in question."

Jen expected Carr to challenge the authenticity of the recording, but Carr just waited as it played. The image, as if looking out through the face shield of Sharpe's suit, was fuzzy in spots and the sound distorted at times. But Jen could see the attacker appear in the hatch, hear Wilmont ordering Sharpe to fire, finally hear Sharpe's acknowledgement of the order, then as the attacker vanished and the hatch slammed shut the recording ended.

Major Hue walked back to the trial counsel's table.

Commander Carr faced Wilmont, her posture somehow poised as if ready to attack. The master chief watched her warily. "Master

Chief Wilmont. How did you know the individual you sighted through Sharpe's suit was in fact an attacker?"

Wilmont seemed startled by the question. "He or she matched what we knew about them."

"And what we knew about them was that the attackers were wearing survival suits like our own, isn't that right, master chief? Where are the identification markers on our suits?"

"The shoulder, the right breast —"

"How clearly could you see the right breast and shoulder of that figure you ordered Sharpe to fire on, master chief?"

"I don't —"

"Weren't they both obscured in whole or part by the coaming of the hatch and other intervening objects?"

"Objection, Your Honor!" Major Hue was on his feet. "Defense Counsel is harassing the witness."

"Your Honor," Carr stated, "I am doing my job of cross-examining the assertions of this witness."

Halstead pointed his finger at Carr, then at Hue. "Keep it civil, both of you. Defense Counsel is enjoined to watch her tone with the witness."

"Yes, Your Honor." Carr spun to face Wilmont again and the master chief almost flinched. "Well, master chief? How certain could you be that the target you identified was the enemy, and not one of your masters-at-arms or another sailor assigned to this station?"

"I knew. You have to make calls in combat. Decisions. You have to make them fast. And people have to obey orders, do what they're told. Otherwise people like Chief Yasmin and Petty Officer Hastings die. And they *did* die."

"Yes, they did," Carr agreed. "Their time of death was established by surviving suit records at zero one forty four. Six minutes before you gave Sharpe an order to fire. Isn't that right, master chief?"

"Objection. Defense —"

"Overruled." Judge Halstead waved to Carr. "Continue, counsel."

"Thank you, Your Honor." Carr paced a bit from side to side, looking to Jen like a shark circling its prey. "Master chief, did you at any time hesitate to give specific directions to those masters-at-arms on the front lines because they were on the scene and you were not?"

"We had a good picture on the command and control circuits. That's all I needed."

"The bodies of Chief Yasmin and Petty Officer Hastings were found in a location inside that hatch, weren't they? The investigation concluded that they'd pushed too far forward, out of contact with the other masters-at-arms, for unknown reasons, most likely because the positions of the attackers and their fellow masters-at-arms were too hard for them to determine." Wilmont frowned. "If they'd survived, they could have been trying to reach safety through that hatch, couldn't they?" Wilmont just stared at Carr.

Hue was on his feet again. "Objection. Your Honor, Defense Counsel is speculating and creating hypothetical situations."

"I agree. Objection sustained. Move on, Defense Counsel."

Carr stopped walking, focusing on Wilmont. "Have you, at any time, then or subsequent to the events of 6 July, asked Chief Sharpe why he didn't obey your order to fire?"

"No," Wilmont answered shortly.

Raising one eyebrow at Wilmont, Carr tapped her rank insignia with one finger.

Wilmont flushed. "No, ma'am."

"Why not?"

"Because in the operational forces we aren't in the habit of explaining our orders! We expect them to be carried out when they're given, without hesitation." Wilmont paused. "A lawyer might not understand that."

Carr smiled at Wilmont in a way that made the master chief suddenly jerk backwards slightly, looking nervous. "You might be surprised what lawyers understand, master chief. To summarize your position, then, orders must be obeyed when given and without questioning, and there are no circumstances, especially in combat, in which it is acceptable to turn a blind eye to a clear order."

Wilmont sat silent, then nodded quickly. "Yes . . . ma'am."

"Do you recognize the 'blind eye' reference, master chief?"

Wilmont gazed back, plainly uncertain.

"Vice Admiral Nelson at the Battle of Copenhagen in 1801," Carr continued. "While Nelson's ships were engaged, his superior officer, some miles distant, hoisted a flag signal ordering Nelson to break off the action and withdraw. Nelson raised his telescope to his blind eye and announced that he could see no signal, then went on to win a decisive victory. He openly and publicly violated a clear order, master chief. You therefore believe Nelson should have been court-martialed, correct? Because he had no alternative but to obey that order, correct?"

Carr had taken a half-step forward with each sentence, and now her face was less than half a meter from Master Chief Wilmont's, her eyes fixed on him. Wilmont was pressing himself hard against the seat back.

"Objection, Your Honor." Major Hue was shaking his head. "Defense counsel is now introducing hypothetical situations into the trial."

Without moving or taking her eyes off of Wilmont, Carr spoke. "Is Trial Counsel prepared to argue that well-documented historical events are inadmissible in this court? If so, I would remind Trial Counsel that the events on this station on 6 July are also well-documented historical events."

Halstead smiled thinly. "Objection overruled."

Wilmont had been trying to look elsewhere, but found his eyes caught once again by Commander Carr's. "Well, master chief? Should Nelson have obeyed that order? Should he have been court-martialed for disobeying it while facing the enemy? Yes or no?"

"I . . . don't know."

"You don't know? Why can't you give me a yes or no answer, master chief?"

"Because I don't know his reasons!"

"You don't know his reasons. Do you know Chief Sharpe's reasons, master chief? No? You never even asked." Carr eyed Wilmont for a long moment while the master chief visibly began sweating, then spun away. "No further questions."

Jen felt a heavy feeling in her gut as she watched Carr walking back to her seat after savaging Master Chief Wilmont. *She never did that to me. Not like that. What if she had?*

Hue was rubbing his forehead again. "No redirect, Your Honor."

Captain Daladros cleared her throat. "Master chief, did you have any qualms about ordering someone on the scene to shoot at a target they were hesitant to engage?"

"No, ma'am. I gave him a clear order." Wilmont was breathing heavily. "I could see clearly enough."

"Even though you weren't on the scene?"

"Yes, ma'am."

Lieutenant Brook leaned forward. "Why did you press these charges, master chief?"

"Because Sharpe's actions were dangerous and negligent, ma'am. I need to know that people under my command will do what they're told, and they need to know that obedience to orders is expected of them."

Brook's expression was hard to read. "Exactly as they're told?"

"Yes, ma'am."

Hue waited until Master Chief Wilmont had left the courtroom, then rose again. "The prosecution rests."

The court recessed for lunch and Jen ran out to grab food while Carr kept working. "Sandwich, ma'am?"

"Thanks." Carr took an absent-minded bite, then gave the sandwich a surprised look. "Bulgur wheat? How'd you know?"

"And herbal tea," Jen said, giving her the drink. "Why didn't you bring up the personal stuff? About that master chief not getting along with Sharpe?"

Carr chewed and swallowed, looking thoughtful. "If that was all I had, I'd use it, but proving personality conflicts are behind charges is very hard to do. The members could decide that the master chief had every right to dislike Sharpe but still believed charging him here was the right thing to do. Or that Sharpe might have disobeyed the order because of a personality conflict, which is no defense at all. It's a minefield I prefer to avoid, especially since it might have brought out the fight between Sharpe and Wilmont, which would have made them *both* look bad."

"You've got them on the run, don't you?"

"Probably. But I never let a wounded enemy escape, lieutenant. We need to finish them off."

"The defense calls as its first witness Lieutenant Junior Grade Akesha Taylor."

Jen watched Taylor walking confidently toward the witness stand. Taylor had worked her way up from enlisted and had served with Paul on the *Michaelson* for a while. Despite her junior officer rank, she was probably the most experienced individual in the room.

Carr stood in an attentive but relaxed posture in front of Taylor. "Are you Lieutenant Junior Grade Akesha Taylor, currently assigned to the staff of Commander, United States Naval Space Forces?"

"Yes, ma'am." Taylor rubbed her brow for a moment. Under the cover of that movement, Taylor gave a surreptitious wink to Jen.

"Were you assigned to evaluate lessons learned from an electronics stand-point after the attack of 6 July?"

"Yes, ma'am." Taylor spoke casually but with total confidence.

"Are you familiar with the signals environment involving the station emergency response forces on 6 July?"

Taylor made a small snort. "Yes, ma'am."

"How would you characterize that signals environment?"

"In polite company, commander?" Taylor asked. "Chaos. Bedlam. Goat-rope."

Carr leaned forward, suddenly intent. "Why? What happened?"

"Two things." Taylor held up one hand with the first two fingers displayed. "First thing, the bozos who attacked us deployed broad-spectrum noise makers. Those things pumped out random messages and signals up and down the frequency range to confuse and jam our own signals." One finger came down. "But our suits could handle some of that because of their comm suite filters. A bigger problem was that the relays and junctions were blown out or fried in a large area of the station and our masters-at-arms had to operate there." Taylor's other finger dropped. "Normally, our suits use very low power signals on very limited frequencies to minimize the amount of RF energy bouncing around inside the station."

"RF energy?"

"Sorry, ma'am, I mean radio frequency energy. The station is shielded to keep radiation out. That means it also keeps radiation in. If everybody and everything was yakking away on high-powered wireless connections this whole station would turn into an economy-sized microwave oven. Great for popcorn, bad for people and equipment."

Carr nodded, her expression serious even though many other people grinned at Taylor's description. "Normally, you said. What happened during the attack?"

Taylor spread her hands. "The relays were gone, or the junctions were gone, or both. Our suits tried to shake hands with the nearest relays so their low-powered signals could be picked up. No joy. So the suits automatically shifted to emergency comm mode, boosting signal strength and changing frequencies. The suits keep doing both until they find a relay to shake hands with." Now Taylor moved her hands rapidly from side to side. "We ended up with high power signals bouncing down the walls of passageways like they were giant transmission channels, leaking through everywhere they could, reflecting here, there and everywhere. And these were signals our suits were supposed to listen to. So they tried, but the signals seemed to be coming from all sides, the real locations couldn't be identified, their strength varied like crazy, and most were distorted or fragmentary." Taylor shrugged. "Goat-rope."

Carr nodded. "We earlier reviewed recordings of the scene from Chief Sharpe's suit during the engagement. That recording was filtered to make it clearer. With the court's permission, the defense would now like that recording run unfiltered, exactly as Chief Sharpe experienced it."

Halstead glanced at Hue, but the trial counsel apparently realized the request was too reasonable to be denied. "The court so orders."

The display winked to life, the now-familiar scene appeared, but this time a constant stream of noise rattled from it and symbology flashed and faded in seemingly random patterns on the heads-up display. Words and phrases could be picked out, as well as occasional sentences, but Jen found herself developing a headache as the cacophony went on. She could still make out Wilmont's orders and Sharpe's reply, but not easily. Finally, Carr turned off the recording. "That was only thirty seconds of the replay," she reminded the members. "Thank you, LTJG Taylor."

As Carr returned to her seat, Major Hue approached Taylor warily. "Lieutenant, don't survival suits contain the means to filter out signals such as we just experienced?"

Taylor nodded. "Sure."

"Then Chief Sharpe could have reduced that noise, could have rendered his operating environment clearer."

"Yeah, major, but –"

"Thank you, lieutenant. Did the system records reveal Chief Sharpe complaining about the comm environment during the engagement?"

Taylor smiled unpleasantly at Hue. "A lot of the words I heard from Sharpe and the other masters-at-arms had something to do with that. I'd be happy to recite some of them if you want, major."

Hue gave Taylor a sour look and shook his head. "That's quite all right. How do you know those words concerned the communications environment?"

"Well, when I hear people saying the 'f-ing circuits are f-ing f-ed up' and 'what the f-ing hell is the f-ing chief trying to f-ing tell us,' then I figure it has something to do with the comm environment."

Chuckles in the courtroom were hastily stifled as Judge Halstead glared around. Hue twisted his mouth, gave Taylor a long look, then started back to his table. "No further questions."

"Defense wishes to redirect," Carr said, standing again. "LTJG Taylor, what were you saying regarding Chief Sharpe's ability to filter out the signals he and the other masters-at-arms were encountering on 6 July?"

Taylor grinned. "I was saying, it has to be done manually, calling up the right subroutines and reassigning functions and priorities. The software can walk you through the process, but it takes a while and it takes your full attention."

"Manually? It requires a lot of time and your full attention?"

"That's correct, ma'am. One of my strongest recommendations was for that system to be totally reworked."

"No further questions."

Lieutenant Commander Nasser nodded to Taylor. "How long would it take you to do such a manual filtering?"

"Me?" Taylor thought for a moment. "In that complex an environment? Five minutes, I guess. I don't do it every day."

"How long would you estimate it would have required one of the masters-at-arms to do it on 6 July in that environment?"

Taylor squinted toward the overhead. "Fifteen minutes? Maybe half an hour. If they didn't get shot while they were figuring out the next step."

Master Chief Kobo spoke next. "Why didn't Colonel Lamont talk about this problem, LTJG Taylor?"

"I don't know. I wasn't here when he talked to you. But I do know the Marines didn't have the same problem. Their combat armor is designed to operate in places where there aren't relays, so their own suits function as relays and junctions for everybody's comms. They also don't use the same frequencies or protocols as Navy suits, so they weren't bothered much by the junk our suits were putting out. To the Marine comm suites it was just so much sailor noise to be ignored."

Kobo looked thoughtful. "Is the rest of fleet staff going to get input to the comm fixes you've proposed?"

"Look me up after this is over, master chief. You'll get a say in it."

Master Chief Kobo settled back, looking contented.

Carr stood up as Taylor left. "Your Honor, the defendant wishes to testify as a sworn witness on his own behalf."

Halstead gave Sharpe a questioning look. "Chief Sharpe, you have the right to make a statement. Included in your right to present evidence are the rights you have to testify under oath, to make an unsworn statement, or to remain silent. If you testify, you may be cross-examined by the trial counsel or questioned by me and the members. If you decide to make an unsworn statement you may not be cross-examined by trial counsel or questioned by me or the members. Are you certain you want to testify under oath?"

Sharpe had risen, too, and nodded firmly. "Yes, Your Honor."

"Then take the stand, please."

Sharpe sat in the witness chair and waited as Commander Carr approached. "Chief Petty Officer Sharpe," Carr began, "tell us your thoughts when you received the order from Master Chief Wilmont to fire at the individual in the hatch."

"Yes, ma'am." Sharpe's expression was as serious as Jen had ever seen it. "The situation was really muddled. Lots of noise, lots of things happening, and no one knew enough about what was going on. I saw the hatch open and I aimed my weapon at the person who appeared in it. I couldn't make out any identification. I hesitated, because I knew we didn't know exactly where all of our own people were. Master chief ordered me to fire and I started to, but I stopped, trying to see if I could make out anything on the target which would ID it as friend or foe. Master chief ordered me to fire again. I said, "aye, aye" and prepared to fire, but stopped again because I couldn't see any weapon, couldn't see any ID, couldn't see anything to tell me who that target was. Master chief came on again and I started to ask how we knew that person wasn't a friendly, and then whoever it was jerked back inside."

Sharpe grimaced. "I had an order. I admit that, but that could have been a friendly, ma'am."

Carr nodded with just a trace of sympathy. "As a member of the armed forces, are you required to obey any and all orders, Chief Sharpe?"

"All orders? No, ma'am. Only lawful orders."

"Lawful orders?" Carr prodded.

"Orders which don't conflict with existing law or regulation," Sharpe recited. "You can't be ordered to rob a bank or mutiny or desert your place of duty, just to cite a few examples."

"Can you be ordered to shoot someone you believe might be friendly?" Carr asked.

"Objection, Your Honor." Before Major Hue could say more, Halstead stopped him with a gesture.

"Defense counsel has every right to question her witness as to his own state of mind, Trial Counsel. Overruled."

Sharpe looked from Halstead to Carr. "No, ma'am. You can't be ordered to shoot one of your own people."

"Did you honestly believe there was a real chance that individual was a friendly, Chief Sharpe?"

"Yes, ma'am, I did."

"No further questions."

Major Hue walked up to Sharpe, his face hard. "Chief Sharpe, how strong was this belief that the target might be a friendly?"

"Strong enough, sir."

"What evidence did you have that the target was friendly? Was there any evidence?"

Sharpe nodded, not intimidated by Hue's pointed questions or attitude. "Yes, sir. A suit which appeared the same as ours and no obvious indicators of hostile action or intent while I was observing that individual."

"Do the sailors under your command routinely decide whether or not to obey your orders, Chief Sharpe?"

"No, sir." Sharpe's lips drew back slightly. "I don't do it routinely either, but there was nothing routine about that situation."

Major Hue watched Sharpe, then shook his head and walked back to his table.

LCDR Nasser gave Sharpe a challenging look. "Chief Sharpe, how often have you disobeyed orders? Lawful or unlawful?"

Sharpe rubbed his lower face, obviously thinking. "Disobeyed, sir? Once, sir. On 6 July."

Nasser glanced at the judge. "He's still under oath, right?"

"That's correct," Halstead replied.

"Just once, Chief Sharpe? In how many years?"

"Twelve years in the Navy, sir."

Master Chief Kobo leaned his chin on one hand. "I got the impression from your boss's testimony that he doesn't like you. Are you a smart-ass, Chief Sharpe?"

"I can be, master chief," Sharpe admitted.

"Do you get the job done?"

"Yes, master chief. I get it done and I get it done right. I've never had a bust thrown out in court and I've never let down the people I work for. Ask anybody."

Kobo's gaze went to Jen for a moment. "I don't think I have to, Chief Sharpe."

Captain Daladros spoke next. "Chief Sharpe, knowing everything that you know now, would you have fired when ordered to fire?"

"Yes, ma'am."

"If the situation somehow repeated exactly, if you knew then only what you knew then, would you fire or not?"

Sharpe considered the question, his face troubled. "I don't know, ma'am."

"You've thought about it?"

"Yes, ma'am. I wasn't certain I was right, it turned out I was wrong, but I don't know if I'd do different if the exact same thing happened again."

Captain Daladros sat back, clearly thinking.

"The defense rests," Commander Carr announced.

Halstead faced Major Hue as Sharpe returned to his seat at the defense table. "Is Trial Counsel prepared for closing arguments?"

"Yes, Your Honor." Major Hue walked steadily to a point facing the members' table. "Your Honor, members of the court, a lot of excuses have been offered in this court today. Excuses like 'it wouldn't have mattered.' 'It didn't make any difference.' 'The situation was confusing.' 'There was noise.' 'The target couldn't be precisely identified.' Every one of those excuses fail the tests to which they must be set. The test of duty. The test of responsibility. The test of discipline. Even the test of team work which Colonel Lamont invoked, because how can a team function if one member takes it upon himself to disregard the instructions of the team leader? Chief Sharpe received a clear, unequivocal order. He acknowledged receiving that order. He didn't carry it out. He didn't even offer an explanation at the time for not obeying the order. The very existence of this station, the lives of everyone on it, were on the line, and Chief Sharpe hesitated in the face of the enemy. That's the bottom line, that's the one thing no excuse can minimize. When his duty made its sternest demands on him, when his fellow personnel needed him the most, Chief Sharpe hesitated. I ask you to find him guilty as to all charges and specifications."

Major Hue sat and Commander Carr walked to about the same place, facing the members. "Your Honor, members of the court, there are indeed serious issues here, but they involve second-guessing of a single action by a single individual and attempts to blow that one action out of proportion. You heard the testimony of Captain Dila and Colonel Lamont. Those who attacked this station did exactly what they were told, even when those orders were clearly wrong and counter-productive, and when deprived of detailed instructions were at a loss. The personnel defending this station had to react in the face of confusion, of lost and damaged systems, of inadequate information, but they did act, and they frustrated the attack on this station. Why? Because we entrust our defense to people who are trained to *think*.

"A military force needs discipline. But it also needs initiative, it also needs wisdom, it also needs common sense. You heard Colonel Lamont, a decorated veteran of combat. *It depends*, he said. Should front-line troops follow exactly the orders they receive from superiors removed from the scene? It depends. Chief Petty Officer Sharpe is being charged with failing to follow an order to fire when he believed his target was a friendly. He could have fired, and avoided these charges. But he is not a robot, not a machine. He is a human being, and in the final analysis we need to ask ourselves what we want defending us – machines which kill without hesitation on order, or humans who sometimes hesitate, sometimes think, sometimes decide that the order they've received may be unlawful, may be wrong."

Carr pivoted to look at Sharpe. "Some of the charges against Chief Sharpe were disproved by the testimony of the prosecution's own witnesses. His failure to fire on one occasion at one possible target did not have any impact on whether or not this station was saved, but his actions as part of the emergency response *team* were important in saving the station. But as Chief Sharpe testified, and as the prosecution did not attempt to refute, he was under no obligation to obey an order he reasonably believed could be unlawful. In the end, that's what this court-martial comes down to, what the members of this court must decide. Do we grant those to whom we entrust our defense the right to think and to decide, or do we insist that they rigidly follow instructions even when they have cause to believe those instructions are wrong? Do we use the intelligence and common sense of our personnel, or do we order them to do exactly as they are told without question? The answers aren't always easy, but that's why we need to offer our personnel the right to use their own initiative instead of insisting on ironclad, no-exception rules. Our enemies have chosen one path. I urge you to chose the other, and find Chief Petty Officer Sharpe innocent as to all charges and specifications."

Captain Halstead looked from the members to the trial counsel's table to the defense counsel's table. "The members will now deliberate. Do you anticipate difficulty in rendering findings, LCDR Nasser?"

Nasser looked to either side at the other members. "No, Your Honor."

"Then this court is closed and will reconvene at ten hundred tomorrow in this same courtroom."

After everyone else had left, Jen turned to Commander Carr. "I didn't realize my presence here would sandbag Major Hue as much as it did."

Carr stretched and smiled. "I hoped for that, and got more than I expected. But the game isn't over, lieutenant. I never celebrate prematurely."

Jen jerked her chin toward the judge's bench. "I was thinking, if they'd just charged Sharpe with disobeying an order, it probably would've got him non-judicial punishment and he would've taken hits there. But they wanted to nuke him."

"You're very likely right, lieutenant. But that's one of the perils of trying to classify too much. The right people, the ones who could've kept this from getting this far, didn't hear about it at all or heard too late to impose a little sanity on the process. Chief Sharpe might have been hammered because of that." Carr yawned. "I'm not even sure what time-zone my body is in. I'll see you in the morning, lieutenant."

"Yes, ma'am." Jen watched Carr leave the courtroom.

"Have the members reached findings?" Captain Halstead asked.

"We have." LCDR Nasser passed over the data pad containing the findings to the bailiff, who carried it to the judge, who studied the pad before handing it back.

"Chief Sharpe," Halstead directed, "will you and your counsel stand up. LCDR Nasser, announce the findings, please."

Nasser gave Sharpe an enigmatic look, then focused back on the data pad. "Chief Petty Officer Ivan Sharpe, this court finds you not guilty as to all charges and specifications."

There was some more legal boilerplate to go through, but eventually Captain Halstead looked around the courtroom once again. "The court-martial is adjourned."

As the judge, the members and Major Hue left the courtroom, Chief Sharpe turned to Jen and saluted her. "Thank you, ma'am."

Jen returned the salute, shaking her head. "You and I both know what Lieutenant Sinclair would have done if I hadn't helped bail you out, Sheriff. You damned well better thank Chief Henga for saving your butt, too."

Sharpe's old grin finally returned. "The woman never listens to me."

"Lucky you. Get back to work, Sheriff. Try to stay out of trouble from now on."

"Yes, ma'am. Please give my regards to Lieutenant Sinclair."

Jen waited while Commander Carr finished wrapping up paperwork with the court, uncertain if her role as assistant had wrapped up as well. When Carr finished and came back to the defense counsel's table she gave Jen a surprised look. "You're free, lieutenant. I'm officially back on leave, while I try to find the quickest shuttle back to Earth."

"I know some contacts who might help," Jen suggested.

"Do you know a decent place to eat while I work those contacts?"

"Fogarty's is okay, if you don't mind being around a lot of ship drivers."

Carr grinned. "Some of my favorite people are ship drivers. Can I treat you to a victory lunch?"

"Thank you, ma'am." They began walking out of the courtroom, Jen struggling with words she knew she had to say. "Commander, Paul always told me that you pulled your punches when you were prosecuting me. I never really believed him."

Carr shook her head in denial, but didn't look at Jen. "I did my duty."

"Which isn't always that easy to figure out, is it? But I saw what you did to that master chief. If you'd hit me like that, with all the stress I was under, I might've fallen apart."

"I doubt that," Carr remarked. "You stood up pretty well on 6 July. I've never thought of myself as being more intimidating than terrorists."

"Don't sell yourself short, ma'am. Anyway, thanks for what you did for Chief Sharpe."

Carr swept away Jen's thanks with a wave of her hand. "I'm still trying to balance the scales, lieutenant. Besides, I wanted to see justice done in this case, too. But if you need me again, you call me. Understand?"

"Yes, ma'am." Jen extended her hand. "Pax?"

"Seriously?" Carr stopped, looking at Jen's offered hand, then smiled and shook it. "Thanks." They started walking again. "How's Paul doing on Mars, by the way?"

"Getting in trouble."

"Big shock."

"Yeah. You heard about the Utopia incident, didn't you?"

Carr nodded. "I saw the transcripts, but I'd love to hear Paul's personal take on things."

"Well, stuff started going wrong as soon as he got to Mars, starting with the surprise he got when he reported in . . ."

ABOUT THE AUTHOR

"Jack Campbell" is the pseudonym for John G. Hemry, a retired Naval officer who graduated from the U.S. Naval Academy in Annapolis before serving with the surface fleet and in a variety of other assignments. He is the author of The Lost Fleet military science fiction series, as well as the Stark's War series, and the Paul Sinclair series. His short fiction appears frequently in *Analog* magazine, and many have been collected in ebook anthologies *Ad Astra*, *Borrowed Time*, and *Swords and Saddles*. The Pillars of Reality is his first epic fantasy series. He lives with his indomitable wife and three children in Maryland.

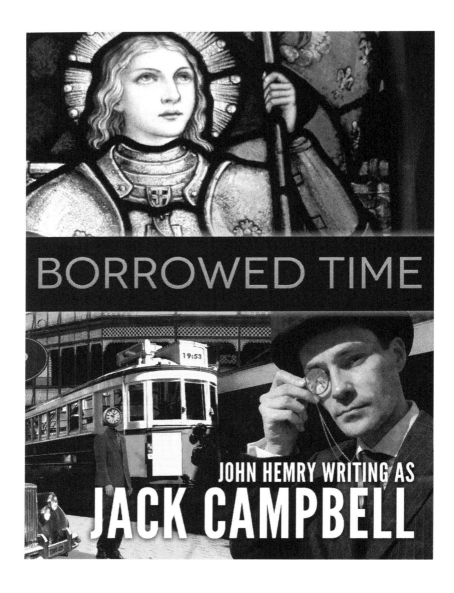

BORROWED TIME

JOHN HEMRY WRITING AS
JACK CAMPBELL

FOR NEWS ABOUT JABBERWOCKY BOOKS AND AUTHORS

Sign up for our newsletter*: http://eepurl.com/b84tDz
visit our website: awfulagent.com/ebooks
or follow us on twitter: @awfulagent

THANKS FOR READING!

*We will never sell or giveaway your email address, nor use
it for nefarious purposes. Newsletter sent out quarterly.